Happy Camper

Sarah L. Young

Ben Yehuda Press
Teaneck, New Jersey

Published by Ben Yehuda Press
122 Ayers Court #1B
Teaneck, NJ 07666
http://www.BenYehudaPress.com

To subscribe to our monthly book club and support independent
Jewish publishing, visit https://www.patreon.com/BenYehudaPress.

Ben Yehuda Press books may be purchased at a discount by
synagogues, book clubs, and other institutions buying in bulk. For
information, please email markets@BenYehudaPress.com.

ISBN13 978-1-963475-24-1 pb
978-1-963475-25-8 epub

25 26 27 / 10 9 8 7 6 5 4 3 2 1   20250630

This book is dedicated to everyone
who has ever questioned whether
they belong at camp.

You do.

Chapter One

Two sturdy-looking wood posts held up the archway sign, with CAMP GESHEM burned into the grain. A banner of white cloth hung just underneath, reading WELCOME HOME, 2010 CAMPERS! in hand-painted blue letters. The dot of the exclamation point was a lopsided Star of David. Beyond the sign stretched endless green and blue, with wooden buildings clustered along the pathway. Teenagers drifted out of minivans and sedans, carrying duffel bags full to bursting as they navigated to their assigned cabins. It was the typical scene you'd expect to see on the first day of camp, and you couldn't have asked for a more beautiful place to spend eight weeks.

As we drove under the sign, I looked at the banner flapping underneath it and thought, *What bullshit.*

I looked out the window as my mom drove deeper into the camp. Most of the signs posted outside the buildings were written in Hebrew, a language I didn't speak and could only barely read. I could already see how tomorrow was going to go: I was going to show up at the arts and crafts building instead of the dining hall for breakfast. Talk about an embarrassing first impression. But the language barrier was the least of my problems; so far, I hadn't seen a single camper who wasn't white, which meant I was going to stand out like a sore Latina thumb. Worse, if this camp was anything like my hometown, I was going to be the only person here who wasn't straight either.

Ordinarily that wouldn't be too bad; I was used to being the only lesbian. But the articles I'd read said that Camp Geshem was one of the worst camps for LGBTQ campers to attend, since it considered itself a Conservative Jewish camp. Even if there were other queer people here, they wouldn't be open about it, and I couldn't be either. The articles made it pretty clear: the people here probably gave bacon more rights than people like me.

We passed by countless girls who all looked exactly like my mother from her old camp pictures. They were all five foot nothing, thin things named Rachel or Sarah or Hannah who went to private Hebrew schools and snuck into the back hall with a guy during free period. The more girls we passed, the deeper my heart sank. There definitely wasn't going to be room for me, tall and big and gay, among their numbers.

"Reina?" My mom at the wheel drew my attention away from the increasingly depressing picture outside. I caught her eyes in the rearview mirror, and she gave me one of those gentle smiles moms make when they think they know best. "I was nervous my first time here, too."

Whatever she said next was lost on me, since I'd heard the story from her and Dad so often. I can sum it up for you: they met at Camp Geshem when they were 14, started dating, kissed under the moonlight in the middle of the lake—the whole shebang. She was *so* sure she could relate to my circumstances, as if she was once a Latina lesbian dropped in an ocean of straight white kids. Too bad she wasn't either of those things, or I'd actually find any advice she was trying to give me useful.

"Reina, are you listening?"

"No."

Instead of staring holes into my head, she merely chuckled. "I'm gonna miss you, kid. The house'll be a lot quieter without you around."

The number of times I had heard that phrase in the last week was starting to reach triple digits. Even Dad had gotten tired of it, telling her over dinner that they would see me after a month anyway. Come to think of it, that was probably the reason he wasn't here today.

We pulled up to Cabin Four in the Chaverim loop; apparently, every section of camp had a cozy name. I opened the car door to a sea of bobbing ponytails and peppy counselors. Two counselors dressed in Camp Geshem staff shirts popped out of the crowd and offered their hands in greeting. "Hey!" said the taller of the two. "I'm Rachel, and this is Sarah. We'll be your counselors this summer. You must be Reina, right?" Rachel said to me.

I nodded and gave her a quick once-over. She was taller than Sarah, but shorter than me. Her waist was nonexistent and her brown hair hung past her shoulders. Sarah was a good head shorter than me and tied her hair in a ponytail. My mom smiled generously at them, and I quickly did the same. "Reina, you're our only new camper this summer," Rachel said. "You get to be the new girl. Isn't that exciting?"

"Super," I replied, grinning. Inwardly, I groaned. It wasn't enough to be stared at for being Dominican; now I was going to get stares for being *new*.

I left my mother to chat with the counselors and retrieved my luggage—three purple floral bags that weren't my idea. Another counselor led me to a shoddy-looking bunk bed marked with a piece of paper with my name on it, written in stylized Hebrew letters. The top bunk belonged to a girl named Tova, who, if the shelves next to the bed were any indication, had already moved in. I surveyed the bunk; thirteen teenage girls lounged around, chatting with each other, painting their nails, and ignoring their parents as best they could.

I rejoined the two counselors and my mother. "Are we late?" I asked, interrupting whatever embarrassing story my mom was telling about my toddler years. "It looks like we're the last ones to arrive."

"Oh, you aren't late," Rachel reassured, though it came off more condescending. "Most of these girls live closer, so they got here earlier."

"They probably all wanted to see their friends," Sarah added. "You should have seen the line this morning to get into camp. It was completely backed up! I can't blame them, though. When I was a camper, I was one of the first to get here and the last to leave."

My mother laughed. "I know the feeling. I was the same."

"Oh-em-gee, you're an alumnus?" Rachel asked, impressed. I rolled my eyes, but fortunately she couldn't see me.

"That's right," my mom said proudly. "I came here for six years. My husband came here too. We started dating a week into his first summer."

"Wow," Sarah said, awe coloring her voice. "You guys are a Geshemarriage?"

I must have groaned loud enough for my mom to hear me, because she glared at me before launching into the story she'd told me all my life: how Dad had offered Mom a rose during the first week, and by the time Shabbat had ended they were dating.

As she dazzled the counselors with her positively *fascinating* love story, I set about unpacking. Mom had definitely put too much in there, but it was my fault for letting her pack instead of just doing it myself. There wasn't enough room on the remaining shelves, so I stuffed excess clothing and bedding into one duffel bag and crammed it under the bed. The only other thing I really needed to do was to make the bed, so I grabbed what I needed and got to work.

By the time my mother had finished telling her story, my bed was made, my empty duffels were tossed up into the rafters, and my stuff was more or less put away. My mother led me outside to hug me goodbye, leaning her head on my shoulder.

"Be good, and at least try to have fun, alright?" she murmured. She looked sad, so I nodded. "Remember, even though all those girls are Sarahs, you're Reina. 'Sarah means princess, but Reina means queen.' I know you'll have fun if you allow yourself to. I love you, sweetheart."

"I love you too, Mom." It was a little hard to reassure her, since I'd never been away from home before. Don't get me wrong, I was ready for a change; I just wasn't sure this was the right one for me.

Mom dabbed at her eyes and walked back to the car. I refused to look back as the sound of crunching gravel got fainter. Well, it was official. I was all alone, in the middle of nowhere, with a bunch of white Jews who probably thought salt was a spice and thought I didn't belong because I liked kissing girls. What the hell had I gotten myself into?

Back inside the cabin, the campers and counselors were sitting in a circle on the floor. After a bit of awkward shuffling, I found a spot in the circle, though it made it less of a circle and more of a sad oval that looked like it had been drawn by a three-year-old.

"Welcome to Camp Geshem!" Rachel said with way too much enthusiasm. She was met with an equal if not greater amount of enthusiasm from the campers, who cheered and clapped and stamped their feet.

"We have some time before our swim tests," Sarah said after the noise died down, "so Rachel and I thought that we could do…"

Oh no. Don't say it.

"Some icebreakers to get to know each other!"

Oh *no*.

Sarah's mind-blowing original icebreaker idea was to go around in a circle and offer up our names and favorite ice creams. The names were a mix of white and Hebrew; Irene, Tova, Rosie, Anne, Hadassah, Sasha, Amanda… There was no way I was going to remember them all. I was still trying to figure out what went wrong with Amanda's crappy dye job when I realized everyone was looking at me, and it was my turn to go.

I cleared my throat. "I'm Reina, and—"

"That doesn't sound like a Hebrew name," Tova said loudly, interrupting me. A few of the other girls murmured among themselves, and my face flushed.

"It's not," I said, keeping my voice carefully even. "It's Spanish. It means 'queen.' My parents adopted me when I was two. My favorite ice cream is—"

"Do you speak Spanish?" the girl next to me said, cutting me off.

"Sort of?" I replied, patience thinning. "It's technically my first language, but I know English better since that's mainly what my parents taught me. I still know enough to get by, though. My favorite ice cream is chocolate chip cookie dough." I sat back, looking around at the circle. "Any other questions?"

The silence was heavy and awkward.

Finally, the girl next to me said, "Sorry. That was probably kinda insensitive to ask. I didn't mean to put you on the spot." She gave me a warm smile, and then turned back toward the circle. "Everyone, I'm Talia."

I watched Talia as she gushed about her favorite ice cream (mint chocolate chip). She didn't wear any makeup, unlike most of the other girls, and her dark hair hung in loose curls. Her cheeks were flushed with natural excitement, and her eyes sparkled. Her shirt promoted some band I'd never heard of. I made a mental note to ask her about it later.

The rest of the introductions were uneventful. Shelly, Eliana, Hayley, Maya, and finally Rachel professed their love for their chosen preferred frozen treat, with the exception of Maya, who said she didn't eat ice cream because "sugar is bad for your health." This was met with some friendly ribbing, which Maya took with a broad grin. Evidently this wasn't the first time she'd voiced her opinion. "It's great to see you guys getting along so well!" Rachel exclaimed, with Sarah nodding by her side. "Unfortunately, we don't have any more time for icebreakers since it's time for swim tests and lice checks. We'll do some after those, okay?" She was met with thirteen nodding heads. "Alright, go change." I kept my eyes laser focused on the floor as we began to change. I knew how fast a rumor could spread from an accidental glance, and I didn't want to risk it. I changed from the bottom up, leaving my shirt for last to avoid any flashing. As I turned, I caught my reflection in the window; chubby, tan, and completely out of my element. The navy blue bathing suit put all the things I didn't like about my body on display, and the little white daisies sprinkled across the nylon fabric didn't really help distract from it. There wasn't much I could do, so I grabbed beach gear and headed for the door.

"Hold it," Rachel said, blocking the door. "Sunscreen?"

I chuckled. "I'm Dominican," I said, like that explained it. She gave me a flat look, so I continued, "I have dark skin, so I don't get burnt. You know, more melanin means no sunburn? I don't need sunscreen."

Rachel rolled her eyes. "One, that's a myth. Two, it's a camp rule. Sarah and I are in charge of you for the next two months; we're like your moms. Not that we're together, I mean." I snickered, but she glared at me and continued. "You're our responsibility, so if you end up with sunstroke or a bad burn, it's on us. We have to make sure that everyone is safe, and part of that is proper sun protection. Got it? So go put it on, and forget about the whole mom thing," she finished.

I grumbled in protest, but I slipped back inside to apply my sunscreen. By the time I finished, nearly everyone else had finished changing and sunscreening and had left the cabin. I wondered if they would leave without me, but when I got outside the group was still waiting for the stragglers. I was grateful for that, since I knew I would have gotten lost without them. We kept waiting for the last girl to leave the cabin, and we all started walking toward the lake.

The others drifted naturally into clumps, chatting among themselves. I didn't have any friends here, so I found myself at the back of the group. I craned my neck to get a look at the scenery. The clouds were a little darker than when I got here, but the sun was still shining and felt good on my skin. I looked ahead at the other girls and was pleasantly surprised to see that Talia was only a few steps ahead of me. I still wanted to know more about the band on her shirt from before, so I sped up a bit until I fell into step alongside her.

"Uh, hey," I said. She glanced over at me and smiled, but nothing more. "It's my first year here," I continued. "What about you? How long have you come here?"

Talia tilted her head, hair curling into the hollow of her collarbone, as she considered. "This is my fourth year," she replied after a moment. "My whole family went here too, so it's kinda become a tradition. It's awesome, I think you'll love it." She seemed to size me up, eyes flicking up and down my figure. She absently curled a lock of hair between her fingers.

"I like the shirt you had on before," I said, trying to fill the awkward silence. "I don't think I recognized the band, though. What kind of music is it?"

Talia looked puzzled for a moment, and then her brows smoothed out in understanding. "It's a Jewish a cappella group that my sister leads at her college, called the Tone Commandments. They sold some T-shirts and stuff so they could afford to produce a new CD last year." I watched her as she chatted some more about the different covers the group had done and the concerts she had gone to. There was something about how her eyes lit up when she was excited, and how she moved her hands to emphasize her words. She was lovely in an effortless sort of way, like the sun just before it finished setting.

I registered that she had stopped talking and I reached for a new question, looking away like I hadn't been drinking in her every detail. "Is the group any good? Not that I think it's bad!" I said hurriedly. "I mean, a cappella is great, I love listening to it, but it's hard and not all groups are *good*, you know?"

She laughed a little, and the tension building up in my shoulders settled. "I know what you mean," she assured. "I love a cappella, but not every group is good at it. There's one group at my school—this all-boys group called the Testostertones. The only thing they have going for them is their name." She rolled her eyes. "Middle school boys aren't exactly known for their vocal talents."

I giggled at that. "Do you sing?" I asked. *Even just her talking voice sounded like a song*, I thought.

"I used to." Talia glanced at her feet. "I got really bad stage fright when I went up in front of strangers, though. I stopped singing and picked up cello instead—that way I could still do music, but blend more into the background, you know?" I didn't really know what to say, so I simply nodded. "I think my parents were disappointed, though, because my siblings all sing." She smiled at the ground, something bitter twisting her expression. "Mark, the oldest—he's always sung everywhere he could. School, synagogue, community choirs, everywhere. He's amazing. Adina can sing too, but she's not as good as him. I think it eats at her a little bit. She always says she's happy for him but seems a little jealous."

I stared at Talia, at a loss for words. I grew up as an only child, so the dynamics of a family with a lot of kids were a total mystery. Before I could come up with a response, she cleared her throat and pointed at a large building we were passing on the road. "That's the main mess hall, where we eat," she said. Her voice had a fake chipper tone to it. "Sorry about that, I have a habit of oversharing to total strangers." She sounded embarrassed.

"It's okay," I said quickly, and she looked up at me, eyebrows raised a bit. "I mean, if anything, it's my fault. I had no idea that question was so heavy, and I didn't mean to bring up bad memories. Plus… you know." I shrugged. "We don't have to be strangers. We're in the same bunk, but I'm new and everyone else isn't, so it's been kind of lonely so far. Everyone is just talking to their old friends."

Talia gave me a bit of a sad smile. "I know how you feel, believe me. My best friend didn't come back this summer, and I wasn't really close to anyone else here." She looked at the backs of all our other bunkmates, split off in twos or threes, chattering away about the latest hit song or new movie. "It's pretty weird, you know? Like being alone in the middle of a crowd. I can't even call 'em strangers since we've all been here before." She chuckled a little, but there was something sorrowful on the edge of it that tugged at my heart.

Why not? I thought. *It's not like anyone else has said so much as a word to me that wasn't forced through a stupid icebreaker.*

"Well, you need a friend, and I need a friend, and we're both hanging out in the back like a couple of losers," I said. She looked at me quizzically, and I lost my train of thought. "So…

you know, maybe since we're both empty in the friend department, we could... help each other out?" She was grinning helplessly now, and I felt my face heat up. "I mean—! We don't seem to hate each other off the bat, so we could at least give it a shot, and the alternative is being lonely for eight weeks, right?"

Talia laughed, and to my relief, it sounded like she was laughing with me, not at me. "Alright," she said, chuckling. "Let's be friends, then." She looked ahead at the rest of the group, and I saw her gaze straying to a few of the girls who had taken each other's hands. Then she smiled at me and offered her own hand. I took it, eager. Her palm was warm and soft. We walked like that all the way to the beach, chatting about favorite songs and movies. I was pretty sure I had a goofy smile the whole time, but I didn't really care. Finally, something was actually going right in this stupid camp.

We reached the lake and joined a line of kids after setting our towels on the sand. Another counselor, college-aged maybe, worked his way down the line, scribbling notes on a clipboard. He instructed kids on how to complete their swim test, in a droning tone that sounded like he would rather be anywhere but here. *Me too, buddy,* I thought as he came to us.

After getting our information, the counselor rattled off some instructions like he'd been doing all day. "Three laps in Section B," he said, jabbing his pencil toward a marked-off section of the lake. "Front crawl, freestyle, whatever suits you. Just no fancy stroke, and *please,*" he said, giving a slightly pained look, "don't try diving—the water's not deep enough." We nodded, and he moved on to the next group of campers.

"Someone must've tried diving," Talia murmured, and she grinned when I snickered.

"We don't have swimming every day, do we?" I asked as we started walking toward our assigned lake section.

Talia shook her head. "If we did, the whole camp would smell like lake water. Why, you don't like swimming?"

It was my turn to shake my head. "I like swimming, I hate swimming *lessons,*" I explained. "Like, I don't need to know what angle I need my legs to be at or the exact arc my arm should make out of the water. This is summer camp, not the Summer Olympics. Plus, you know, wet hair is pretty cold."

Talia laughed in a way that reminded me of tinkling bells. "The younger kids have lessons every day, I think, since the camp wants to make sure everyone knows how to swim. I think there's a Jewish saying about it?"

Some bit of trivia from my Sunday school classes floated into my brain. "Something about dads being responsible for teaching their kids to swim?" I ventured.

"I think that was it!"

I grinned. "Religious school comes in handy after all. Score one for the new girl."

"So, did anyone tell you what activities we do everyday?" I shook my head, and Talia lit up. "Well then, while we wait, why don't I give you a quick rundown of the ins and outs of Camp Geshem?"

I nodded, and she started talking, telling me the difference between fun and boring activities, which counselors were the friendliest, and which girls were best to avoid at all times. As we shuffled forward in line, awaiting our turn to take swimming tests, it struck me that I hadn't felt sour since I had started talking to Talia. Maybe the next two months wouldn't be so bad after all.

Chapter Two

The lake emptied of campers as the swim tests concluded, and Talia and I walked back together, wrapped in towels to stave off the post-swim-test chill. The wind, which had been gentle and cool earlier, now threatened to strip the leaves from the trees, and pushed at our backs as if urging us toward the shelter of our cabin. After changing into dry clothes, Rachel and Sarah called for a reassembly, so we all sat in a circle once more, though when I sat next to Talia, this time it was a bit more purposeful.

"What did you think of your swim tests?" Rachel asked the group. The response was a unanimous "Cold," which she seemed to think was funny. "Well, while you warm up, why don't we get back to those icebreakers from earlier? Does everyone know how to play two truths and a lie?"

Shelly, an Israeli girl, raised her hand. "I don't."

"It's an easy game," Sarah explained. "When it's your turn, say two things about you that are true, and one that's false. Then the rest of us have to guess which thing you said is the lie. Easy enough, right?" Heads bobbed around the circle. "Great. I'll go first. I went vegan for a year, I've been skydiving, and..." She gave a sly smile. "I've been arrested at least once."

She was met with amused laughter and a chorus of votes for her third statement. Once the circle quieted down, Sarah grinned and said, "To tell the truth, I've never been skydiving." She waited a few beats for the understanding to kick in, and then went on. "There was a peaceful protest in Israel at the Western Wall, where women protested against not being allowed to wear prayer garments by... well, wearing them. The police arrested a bunch of people, including me, but we just sat in the local precinct until the American embassy got us out. Best college essay topic ever."

A few girls clapped in response, though whether it was out of awe or amusement was anyone's guess. The whole circle started buzzing, each camper racking her brain to come up with the most unbelievable truth about themselves. As my turn neared, I could feel my stomach twitch with anxiety. I didn't have any wild, unbelievable stories—none that I could safely tell without giving away some very crucial information. I watched Amanda proudly give her three statements, and pushed down a stab of unwanted envy. *How does it feel,* I wondered, watching her, *to be able to talk about yourself truthfully without having to hide anything?*

My turn came exactly when I expected it: before I was ready. The number of eyes turned on me made heat prick under my skin. "Well, uh, I've never been away from home by myself before," I started. *Argh, that's obviously true, but it sounds so pathetic! Maybe people won't believe it because it's TOO pathetic...?* "And... I got a belly button piercing when I was thirteen. And..." *Think, think, think!* "I failed seventh grade Spanish."

The room lapsed into silence. Even Rachel and Sarah glanced at one another quizzically, like they couldn't quite believe the lame set of answers I'd come up with. The quiet stretched on into discomfort, and there was no sound other than the wind rattling the trees outside.

Finally, Tova spoke up. "I mean, it's got to be the last one, right?" she said, looking around the room. "Like, you *said* you spoke Spanish. And that it was your first language. So that one's got to be the lie."

Each girl around the circle murmured an agreement, and the silence melted away like butter on a hot day. I felt the tension slide out of my shoulders as I looked Tova in the eye and proudly said, "Actually, you're wrong. I was adopted when I was really little, so I didn't actually learn a lot of Spanish until I got around to learning in school." I shrugged. "I speak it more like an American, and I failed one quarter in seventh grade."

Tova squinted at me. "So what was the lie then?"

"My parents approved of a belly-button piercing when I was thirteen, but I never went through with it," I replied. "I'm not a big fan of needles."

More silence, though it wasn't nearly as long as the first one. Amanda was the first to break it, giggling into her hand. "Dang, Reina!" she said. "You got us good!"

One by one, the other girls also began to laugh a bit. It sounded good-natured, and I decided to take it as that, grinning along with the rest of the circle. This was shaping up to be a much more pleasant afternoon than I had anticipated.

FLASH.

And the lights went out.

BOOM.

And the floor shook.

Someone screamed—I wasn't sure who. I couldn't see the circle of girls in front of me, though I was sure they were there. The only light came from the window, dull and elusive, which started rattling as the first sheets of rain slapped at the panes. All at once, the entire room descended into clamorous chaos.

"Everyone stay calm!" someone shouted over the noise. I recognized it as Sarah, though she didn't sound very calm herself. "Quiet down, please! I need you all to listen to me." It probably took longer than she wanted it to, but the room's noise eventually died out. "Okay," Sarah said. "First priority is that we need to stay safe." A bright, artificial light shone out of her phone, with Sarah's face illuminated from beneath. "Everyone get to your beds, alright? We'll help you out with some light."

By the light of Rachel and Sarah's phones, we all managed to get to our beds. Once they had ensured their campers were in bed, they got into theirs as well. Sarah put her phone face down on the covers so the light could more or less reach the rest of the room. "We're okay," she assured the room. "When it comes to storms like these, what's important is that we get into our beds right away. They're positioned to keep us safe and away from the doors and windows so we don't get hit by any falling trees. So all we have to do is stay in our beds, okay?" She definitely sounded like she was trying to be a leader, but I'm pretty sure I wasn't the only one that heard the tremor in her voice. She was just as scared as the rest of us.

Thunder echoed around the otherwise silent cabin. The other campers' faces, grim and terrified, were only visible in the half-second flashes of occasional lightning, like the world's slowest strobe light. Though the world was far from quiet, the silence in the cabin was absolute.

Well, almost absolute.

"So," a voice I recognized as Talia's said, "how's everyone's first day going?"

A few of the girls bleated out nervous laughter. "I've been going here for years," one said, "but there's never been a storm like this."

"Yeah, this is pretty unusual," Talia agreed. "But one that's this strong is bound to blow itself out pretty fast. In the meantime, we should pass the time somehow. Anyone got any ideas?" She was met with silence, but this was less nervous and more awkward.

"Sing-along, then. Any objections?" When no one objected, Talia began to sing. It was soft, and a little uncertain, but Old MacDonald was a recognizable enough tune, and it didn't take long for a bunch of Jewish girls to fall into the classic call-and-response we were all used to from evening services. When Talia exhausted all possible farm animals, she moved on to other children's songs, with the rest of the cabin following her lead. I didn't realize there were so many verses to Wheels on the Bus, or that there was more than one verse to Mary had a Little Lamb, but I followed along as best I could.

Eventually, though, Talia's repertoire of children's songs ran dry. For a few moments, I wondered if the oppressive silence was going to return. Instead, Talia took a deep breath. "Raindrops on roses and whiskers on kittens…"

The effect was immediate. The entire cabin jumped in without missing a beat, and for the first time I could hear real smiles in their voices. Even better, Talia's voice got more confident bit by bit, putting more force behind each note. The mood in the cabin was actually starting to lighten up a bit.

Then lightning flashed so bright that a few girls shouted, and the spots hadn't even begun to fade from my eyes before a clap of thunder shook the cabin. It sounded like someone had set off a bomb mere inches away. More than one girl burst into tears, and someone stuttered her way into the Shema, a daily prayer that was also whispered in the moments just before death.

"That is enough!" Rachel called in the darkness, a bit sternly. "Girls, we are *not* at Shema level, do you hear me? We're going to be fine." She paused a moment. "If you want, I can lead some prayers for thunderstorms." That earned a few nervous chuckles.

A voice I hadn't heard yet spoke up. "I understand why you're all worried," Shelly said, "but it's bound to pass soon. A storm of this size will be really good for the plants, and when it passes we can thank God for providing for the local wildlife."

There was silence for a few moments as the cabin processed this perspective. Before anyone could respond, though, lightning flashed outside. A few girls tensed in anticipation, but the thunder didn't come. Ten seconds came and went. Another ten wandered by faster. I did the math in my head, and then said, "The storm is miles away now. We should be fine." Sighs of relief echoed through the cabin.

Rachel's phone chimed. "The camp director seems to agree with Reina," she said. "We're free to go outside. And it'd be a real waste to not take the opportunity, so, I have one quick question: does anyone here know how to take a rain shower?" she asked. No one did, but before she could explain, the lights suddenly came back on. "Awesome!" she said, surveying the girls huddled up on their beds. "Anyway guys, a rain shower is when you put on a bathing suit, go outside with your shampoo, and you take a shower in the rain. You have to do it in a big open space, like a field, which is why you can't do it during a thunderstorm. Once it passes, though, if it's still raining, it's the absolute perfect time for a rain shower. Anyone feel like getting clean?" she asked.

Her question was met with a resounding yes from all of the girls who, without being asked to, got off of their beds and started to put on their still-damp bathing suits. We all took our shampoo bottles off of the shelves we had just placed them on, and together we went outside for our first ever rain showers. On the field, we splashed around in the puddles. We ran through the slippery wet grass, went mud-surfing—as one girl said it was called—and eventually put the shampoo in our hair and then let the rain wash everything away. It was perfect.

After all, it wasn't every day you got to dance in the rain.

In the midst of the shouts of excitement, I found myself next to Talia, who was entertaining herself by sinking her toes deep into the mud. "That was really brave of you," I said.

Talia looked up. "What was?"

"The sing-along." I shrugged. "You weren't… y'know, scared about singing in front of people?"

Talia chuckled. "Nah, the dark made it easy. Besides, I wasn't performing, just trying to lift spirits. It didn't matter how my voice sounded."

"Well, you definitely made everyone feel better. I think even the counselors didn't know what to do." I gestured to Rachel, who was in the middle of giving Shelly a light scolding for splattering Amanda's face with mud. "I know they're supposed to be taking care of us, but they're kids, too."

Talia watched the counselors for a moment, and I took the opportunity to admire how her hair caught the glow of the sun as it peeked out from behind the clouds. "If I made a difference," she finally said, "then I'm happy. A little bit of good is better than no good at all. *Tikkun olam* and all that, right?"

"Right." I grinned.

Talia turned back to me and smiled. "Thanks," she said, voice soft. "For—well, honestly, for talking to me earlier. I wasn't really looking forward to camp this year ever since I found out Sammy couldn't make it. I was scared I was going to be alone, or have no one to talk to, and…" She dug her fingers into her arm. "Well, I hate feeling like the odd one out. So…" She smiled again, eyes full of warmth. "Thanks."

"Alright girls, let's get changed for dinner!" Sarah shouted. The bunk clumped together and started toward the cabin. I took up the rear, mostly because my brain was short-circuiting, and my heart was threatening to snap my sternum in two. It was lucky that Sarah had rallied the group when she did, because otherwise I would have said something *really* intelligent back to Talia, like "That's what best friends are for!" or "Hhhhhhhh-hhhhng…" or even "No problem, wanna hold hands under the dining table and have a heartfelt conversation under the stars?" Instead, I kept my mouth shut and followed my bunkmates down the road.

I was starting to figure out why I found my gaze wandering to Talia more often than not, why I found her voice so charming to listen to, why my stomach twisted in a knot when she smiled so warmly in my direction. I was fully aware of how bad it could break if it got out I was a lesbian, and yet here I was, openly crushing on the most beautiful girl I'd seen in my life.

Don't get ahead of yourself, I told myself during dinner, tuning out the idle chatter from the rest of my bunk. *It's not safe to be yourself here. This place won't be kind to you if you show them who you really are.* I caught myself looking at Talia again, who was relating an anecdote from another year at Geshem, and I pointedly looked in a different direction. *Besides, she chose to come here. She's probably straight too. She just latched onto you because her usual best friend isn't here. That's all.* It was a bitter pill to swallow, but one that I had to if I wanted to survive all eight weeks of Camp Geshem.

It wasn't like I wasn't used to the feeling. The only people who knew were my parents and a few of my goyish friends from school. Nobody from the synagogue—way too risky. Even my extended family didn't know—I'd attended enough Thanksgivings to know that it would be a bad idea to bring it up to uncles and cousins. I knew what it was like to lock myself in the closet. I knew what it was like to cut away bits and pieces of myself, to fit in whatever box was necessary. It was fine.

Except... it wasn't fine, not really. I had barely been out of the closet—if only partially—for a year; the idea of having to crawl back into it so soon was enough to make me shudder. I didn't want to go back to the misery of before—the misery of hiding, of shame, of not being quite what the world wanted me to be. I hated feeling like a puzzle piece that didn't fit. I just wanted to be *comfortable* for once, and it was looking like the next eight weeks were going to be anything but.

It was drizzling as we walked back to the cabin, as if the weather was mirroring my mood. *It isn't fair.* Just a few hours earlier I had been happier than I had dared hope to be at Geshem. Now I was wallowing in self-inflicted isolation, dealing with turmoil that I couldn't speak about with anybody.

We turned the corner and I saw the glow of the lights in the camp's office building in the distance. My steps faltered just a bit; it wasn't too late. I could run down, demand that they call my parents, and get out of this nightmare before it got started. I could be home by tomorrow afternoon. The temptation was so strong that I took a step toward the office before I realized what I was doing.

A warm hand grabbed mine, and I jerked out of my panicky haze. Talia was looking at me, brow furrowed. "Reina, c'mon," she said. "The cabin's this way. Don't tell me you're already getting turned around?" Her voice had a slight teasing lilt to it, but her expression was good-natured and having her eyes on me made me want to melt on the spot.

"Right," I said after a moment. "Cabin's this way."

"We're gonna get left behind; hurry up!" Talia laughed, and she half-dragged me to catch up with our cabin mates, away from the office and the prospect of a call home.

Did I really want to call my parents? Did I really want to leave?

Sarah means princess, but Reina means queen, I remembered.

No, I decided, looking down at Talia's hand in mine. I didn't.

Chapter Three

"Do you play basketball?" Talia asked.

I squinted at her for a moment. Breakfast had only just started, and I was still in the process of waking up. Hadassah, one of the girls from our bunk, wore a hopeful expression that exactly matched Talia's.

"Not really," I replied. Talia and Hadassah both groaned, shoulders slumping, and my gut twisted a bit.

"It's not like you have to be good at it," Hadassah tried.

"Oh, well in *that* case, I can swish three-pointers like Michael Jordan." I demonstrated my impeccable skill by tossing a used napkin at the nearby trash bin. It bounced off the rim and joined the rest of the greasy paper and plastic forks.

"C'mon," Hadassah pleaded. "You just have to stand there on the court, you don't even need to handle the ball."

"Then why ask me in the first place?"

"Well," Talia said, mouth full of French toast and syrup, "if there aren't enough kids interested in basketball, the camp just doesn't do it." She swallowed. "Like last year. We were short a few campers, so they herded us all into different activities." She made a face. "Like *dance.*"

I perked up a bit. "We can pick dance? I love dance."

"Yeah," Talia sighed. "It's not *my* favorite, though. Way more fun to run around a court than go through some prearranged steps if you ask me."

"Well, if that happens again this year, we can do some prearranged steps together," I tried. Talia rolled her eyes, but she was smiling.

"Fine," she said, "but I'll warn you now, I have two left feet and I'm gonna botch the entire routine. And then we're gonna lose to all the other camps." She pointed a sticky fork at me. "You'll be the reason the mighty Geshem empire crumbles. I hope you can handle that weight on your shoulders, Reina."

I raised an eyebrow. "I mean… technically, it'd be *your* fault."

Talia gasped dramatically, slamming a hand to her chest. "How *dare* you!" she cried in mock disbelief. "I am the very lifeblood of this institution! A Geshem baby, no less! I would *never* bring this camp to its knees."

I blinked. "You too? Is that common?"

Talia shrugs. "It seems to be, in my family. My parents met here, and my brother met his girlfriend here. My family's hoping that I'll meet my future husband here one of these summers."

She said it so casually, but I could feel her words settling like cold spikes in my stomach. She was straight. Of *course* she was straight. I was an idiot for hoping for anything different—we were here at Camp Geshem after all, the camp that topped every Worst Camps for LGBTQ Teens list.

"That sure would be something," I said, doing a pretty good job of pretending like my heart hadn't just crumpled like a soda can.

"Wouldn't it?" Talia laughed, and I cursed internally for thinking about how it sounded like tinkling bells.

We took our plates up to the compost area and after scraping all the food off, put them in the receptacle. I gave the camp bonus points for being environmentally conscious.

A few hours later, the Chaverim campers assembled in the gym. The girls and boys clumped separately, with the girls complimenting each other's sports gear and the boys, by my guess, competing to see who could be shoved the furthest before he fell down. I wrinkled my nose; the boys at my school took gym way too seriously, and it looked like Geshem boys were no different.

I could only pray that teams would be separated by gender.

"Hey, Reina!" someone called. I turned around to see one of the girls from my bunk sliding up next to me.

"Uh, hey there," I said. I couldn't remember what her name was, but I *did* remember she said she liked bubblegum ice cream in the icebreakers. "What's up?"

"Oh, not much," Bubblegum tittered. I caught her eyes flicking over to the group of boys. "This is the first time we're gonna do something with the boys. I'm really excited."

"Oh, yeah," I replied. "I don't really want to be on their team, though, if they're gonna be like…" I looked over in time to see one boy attempt to leap over his friend, sending them both crashing to the ground. "…that."

Bubblegum laughed. "Yeah, they can get a little rough, but it's pretty cute, don't you think?"

Oh, I did *not* like where this was going.

I cleared my throat and forced a laugh. "Yeah, guess so."

"Which one's your type?" Bubblegum's eyes glittered as she leaned in, pressing into my space.

Ugh. "I mean, I haven't met any of them, so…" I tried, but Bubblegum cut me off.

"Yeah yeah, but which one's your *type?*" she said. "Y'know, who do you think is cutest?" I stared at her, and she must have mistaken my incredulous look for concern, because she waved a manicured hand. "Don't worry," she giggled. "I won't go after him, I promise."

Great. And here I thought the day couldn't get any worse. I scanned over the crowd of boys; most of them were roughhousing, but one boy hovered on the edge of the crowd. He looked a bit mousy, with tousled hair and large glasses. I pointed at him. "Uh, that one. He's… totally my type."

Bubblegum followed my finger, and I caught her lip curling

in disinterest before her expression hurriedly rearranged into something resembling curiosity. "Him? Hmm, I don't know him," she mused. "He must be new, like you." She clapped her hands together. "I'll introduce you to him! The newbies dating would be so cute."

"No wait!" I hissed, reaching for her, but Bubblegum was already gone, skipping toward the boys' group with a mission plain in her posture. I couldn't call her back without her name, so I just watched in flustered horror as she tapped the boy on the shoulder, catching his attention. After they exchanged a few words, Bubblegum waved me over. I reluctantly crossed the distance.

"So," Bubblegum gushed, relishing in what she thought was a meet-cute, "Reina, this is Benjy. And Benjy, this is Reina!" She gestured between us and gave me a big grin and a wink.

I put out a hand. "Nice to meet you, Benjy."

Benjy looked at my hand, and then up at me. Before he could take it, a loud whistle blew, smothering the chatter in the gym in a flash.

A woman stood in the center of the gym, holding a whistle in one hand and a clipboard in the other. She wore a sports visor, a Camp Geshem T-shirt, and grass-stained sneakers. "Bleachers, everyone!" she commanded. The campers dispersed among the metal benches. I tried to get near Talia, but instead I ended up sandwiched between Tova and Irene.

"For those of you who don't know me," the woman announced. "I'm Adina, the sports director of Camp Geshem. How's everyone liking camp so far?" She was met with raucous applause and cheers that rattled around the relatively small gym. "That's what I like to hear!" she grinned. "Let's get you guys sorted into teams, alright?" She consulted the clipboard in her hand. "We've got co-ed... tennis, volleyball, dance, track-and-field, then we've got baseball and basketball for the boys, and softball and basketball for the girls." She gestured to a few of the counselors, who had started passing out slips of paper and a few dozen pencils. "Just rank 'em from first to third and we'll organize teams from there. Hope girls' hoops takes off this year because that's where I hang out." She winked at the crowd.

I glanced over toward Talia, and she was already looking at me, giving me a big grin and a thumbs up. I smiled back but couldn't bring myself to return the thumbs up. I was aiming for dance, after all.

One of the sign-up sheets reached me, and I scribbled down dance as my first choice. There was a tennis racket in my bag courtesy of my mother, so I picked that as a second. As I racked my brain for a third, I caught Talia out of the corner of my eye, huddled over with Hadassah. *Well... they probably won't have enough girls for it anyway.* I scribbled down basketball for my third choice and passed the sheet off to a nearby counselor.

We passed the sheets and pencils forward and went back to talking and hanging out. I booked it away from Benjy and bubblegum ice cream girl and headed toward Talia. She was engrossed in a conversation with Hayley, though, so I kind of wandered around, looking for anyone who wasn't talking to someone else. After a while I realized everyone was talking to each other and I had ended up alone. I walked up to Sarah, one of my counselors.

"What's up, buttercup?" she asked me. I smiled gently.

"Not much, just bored."

"Well yeah, we're just getting set up now. Don't worry, things will pick up once Adina is done assigning everyone to their teams." She flashed me a big smile. "Go make friends!" she suggested loudly. Great, even the counselors didn't want to talk to me.

I wandered around a bit longer until Adina blew her whistle again a few minutes later and we all sat down at the bleachers.

"Congratulations to the girls, you've got yourself a basketball team!" Again, everyone cheered, and this time I did too. I looked over at Talia, who was hugging Hadassah. I felt a little twinge of jealousy, which I knew was stupid because we had just met, and she was probably just being melodramatic when she said we'd be best friends. I wasn't paying attention much until I heard Adina call my name.

I looked up very suddenly, and Adina was motioning for me to come up and join her and two other girls who I guessed were in a different bunk because I didn't recognize them. I walked up timidly, but the girls smiled at me, so I smiled back cautiously.

"Hadassah," Adina called next, and she ran up and stood by me, waving to the rest of the campers.

"Talia," Adina announced, and I smiled at her as she made her way up. Next was Hayley.

Shit, I thought to myself. It was starting to look like a basketball team. Then she called up two other girls who I didn't know.

"Let's hear it for the Camp Geshem Chaverim girls' basketball team!" Adina shouted. I groaned a little, but Talia clapped a hand on my shoulder and suddenly things felt better.

Over the next week or so, I settled into the camp's daily routine, weaving bracelets in arts and crafts, singing songs over the campfire, and trying to remember how to dribble a ball during basketball. It became easier to chat with the girls in my bunk, but I still preferred Talia's company over theirs. Aside from basketball, I sat next to her in Hebrew class—turns out, neither of us could speak it very well. The night always ended with the counselors leading us in the Shema, a traditional routine that

I'd never had the chance to experience.

The time after the Shema was my favorite time of the day because it was when Talia would crawl into my bed to talk and laugh about everything that had happened. I could spend hours listening to her chatter and giggle, but the time we spent together was always painfully short. She had to return to her own bed eventually because of some camp rule that forbade campers from sharing beds. The rules were stupid, and a few girls in the bunk ignored them outright, but to me it was safer to follow them than to risk being outed because I got sloppy. Talia could call me a grump all she wanted—I didn't want to give the counselors a reason to suspect me of the crime of being myself.

It was getting harder to keep my eyes on nothing but the floor when changing, though. If I didn't actively stare at the floorboards, my gaze always wandered in Talia's direction. She was beautiful in more ways than one; her laugh sounded like wind chimes, her eyes twinkled like stars, and her smile made my heart flutter in bliss. She was amazing, and gorgeous, and I would never be able to tell her how I felt. How I *truly* felt. It didn't even matter if, by some paper-thin chance, she returned my feelings. Camp Geshem was too big of a wall to surmount.

Every Friday, the campers were free from lunch onwards to prepare for the Sabbath. By the second week, everyone had found their own routines. Some of the girls went all out, plucking eyebrows, smoking out eyeshadow, staining on lip gloss, painting too many layers of polish on their nails, and coordinating the perfect outfit to draw some boy's attention. Around an hour before we were supposed to gather to welcome the Sabbath bride, most girls had just begun to dress, teaming up with a friend to eliminate every speck of fuzz that dared stick itself to their skirts.

I was already dressed and ready, uninterested in dolling myself up to such an extent. It didn't take much for me to get ready; a French braid to keep my hair in line, a lacy blue dress with fabric that pooled in all the right places, and I was all set. I was so engrossed in the book I was reading that I didn't notice Talia until she tugged on my skirt. I jolted like a surprised cat before realizing who it was, and took a moment to appreciate... well, *her*.

As she stood before me, I had to fight to keep my breath. She was a sight, her curly brown hair half up and half down. She had added just a touch of red lipstick, accentuating her beautiful face. She wore no blush, but her cheeks were pink with excitement. Her maroon velvet dress accented her curves snugly. I thought of what it would feel like to run my hands up and down her body in that dress; to place one hand on the small of her back, brushing the other on her pink cheek, and placing a soft kiss on her red lips. Then I chastised myself, knowing it would never be. I couldn't think that way.

"You look beautiful," I murmured. I sat up and patted the space beside me, inviting Talia to sit. She did so, kissing me on the cheek, and it took all my willpower not to melt on the spot.

"Shabbat Shalom," she replied. Even her voice was gorgeous. "You look great too. Since it looks like we're both ready, do you wanna go for a walk or something? The campgrounds are gonna be virtually deserted until Shabbat starts, so it's really peaceful out."

"Sure, but do we need to let the counselors know or anything?"

Talia shook her head. "No, and even if we were supposed to, this is the only time all week they get to themselves. They won't even realize we're gone."

With that worry erased, I followed Talia out of the cabin and through the grass. Just like she'd said, the campgrounds were quiet, save for the wind rustling in the trees and birds chirping from somewhere up high. It was warm, but not uncomfortably so—a welcome break from some of the hotter days during the week.

"Do you know where we're going?" Talia asked me. When I shook my head, she smiled at me, and the world grew rosier. "Good," she said, and took my hand. Her palm was warm and soft. "Feels good to be out of the cabin. I don't want to be with everyone right now. I just want to be with you." She slowed for a moment, considering. "That's not weird, is it?"

"No," I replied. "I think it's just fine."

Talia giggled and began leading me down the path. I smiled so hard my cheeks began to hurt, and I could swear that even my shadow was smiling. Coming to the camp had been worth it if only for this one moment: alone on the campgrounds, holding hands with a beautiful girl, going wherever our feet may take us. Even if she didn't feel the same way I did for her, this was enough for me.

Hand in hand we walked, with Talia leading me down a dirt trail that skirted around the camp's borders. Every inquiry of where we were going was met with a mischievous, "You'll see." She occasionally stooped to pluck a wildflower and tuck it into my braid with no particular rhyme or reason to the style or color scheme. It didn't matter to me, though; I was going to leave them in anyway. After all, they came from *her*.

Talia turned a corner, and I recognized our destination; it was a small bonfire pit on a hill overlooking the water, where we'd taken swim tests on the first day of camp. I hovered, expecting to walk down to the water, but instead Talia sat down on one of the logs surrounding the fire pit. I followed suit, dropping onto the log only a few inches from her. She stared out at the water down the hill before speaking again.

"I've always loved this view," she said. "It's so peaceful, especially just before Shabbat. The sun is just starting to set, and it reflects off the water. It's… nice." She took my hand again and we sat in silence, watching the sun dip lower and lower toward the horizon. After what seemed like an eternity, Talia broke the silence. "I… I need to talk to you about something *really* personal. It's something I've never told anyone else, but I want to tell you. Just… you need to promise me a few things first, okay?"

"Er, okay…?" I wasn't entirely sure what was going on, but the air had shifted and Talia's grip had gone sweaty. Whatever this was, she was nervous beyond compare.

"First," she continued, her voice trembling a bit now, "you have to promise to keep it a secret. And I mean, from *everyone.* Especially anyone at the camp. You with me so far?" I nodded, and she kept going. "Second, you have to promise that you'll stay my friend. Okay?"

I stared at her, dumbfounded. "Talia, what's this abou—"

"Just promise me." Talia squeezed my hand and she looked at me. With a jolt, I realized she had tears in her eyes. I'd only known Talia for a couple of weeks, but she didn't strike me as the kind of person that cried easily. Without thinking, I leaned forward and pulled her into a hug.

"Whatever it is," I murmured, "I won't tell anyone. It'll stay between us. And no matter what it is, I won't stop being your friend. I promise."

Talia sniffled, wiping her face with the heel of her hand, and I let her go. Her face was flushed, though whether it was from embarrassment or nerves I couldn't tell. She took a few deep breaths, as though psyching herself up, and began.

"Do you… well, do you know what the term pansexuality means?"

"Er, no," I said. "Could you explain it to me?"

Talia flushed even darker, but she pushed on, undeterred. "Pansexuality is an orientation that refers to being attracted to people of all genders. You with me so far?"

"I think so," I said after a moment. "What do you mean by 'all' genders, though? Aren't there just two?"

Talia smiled a bit at me, and I noted the tension slipping out of her shoulders. "It's a bit more complicated than that," she said. "Everyone knows men and women—that's what we call the gender binary, because it's either one or the other. But some people don't feel comfortable being put into one of those two categories; instead, they exist outside the gender binary. 'Non-binary' is the typical umbrella term for those people, but a lot of genders exist underneath that umbrella." Her hands moved as she spoke, painting a picture only she could see. "There's a lot to it, so much more than I imagined. I gave a presentation to my grade about it and everything." She paused and looked a tad sheepish. "Sorry if I'm talking too much."

"You're fine," I assured. "I've read about some of this online, but not in this kind of detail. Keep going."

"Right." Talia smiled at me. "So someone who's pansexual is… just a person who is capable of being attracted to almost anyone. Are you with me so far?"

I nodded. "You explained it pretty clearly."

Talia looked a bit relieved at how well I was absorbing the information. "Thanks," she said. "I just wanted to make sure we were on the same page before…" She trailed off, glancing toward the water again.

"Before?" I prompted.

"I'm pansexual," Talia blurted out. As soon as the words left her lips, she twisted away from me, pulling away as though she'd been stung. I could only stare at the back of her head, stunned. I hadn't been sure where this was going, but this sure wasn't it.

At first my heart started beating fast. I should have been excited knowing I wasn't the only one keeping such a big secret, but instead I felt panicked. Why was she telling me this? Didn't she know she could get in trouble? How should I respond? Could I tell her that I was gay too? Was that safe? Maybe there were others.

After what was only probably two minutes of thinking but felt like two years, I reached out and put a hand on Talia's back. She jerked in surprise. "Thank you for trusting me enough to tell me something so personal," I murmured. "It doesn't change how I feel about you."

Talia turned back to me, crying harder than she had before. I opened my arms and she buried herself into them, pressing her face into my shoulder as I rubbed her velvety back. I felt her fingers curl into the back of my dress and she clung to me, sniffling and muttering something about her eyeliner running.

"If you were planning on coming out to me, you should have worn waterproof eyeliner," I pointed out.

"Shut up, I'm emotionally recuperating," she responded, voice muffled. I had to laugh a bit at that. "I don't know why, I just felt like I could trust you."

"As long as we're telling secrets, wanna know mine?" I asked.

Talia lifted herself off my shoulder; her eyeliner hadn't smeared nearly as bad as it could have. "Sure," she said.

"You have to promise that you'll keep it a secret," I went on, "and that you'll stay my friend after."

Talia's brow furrowed. "Wait, are you saying…"

"I'm a lesbian."

It took Talia about three seconds of blank staring to process this before her face broke out into a grin so wide it pushed her cheeks into her eyes. She lunged at me with a hug so fast we both toppled over in surprise, and I went down with a yelp.

"My *dress!*" I shouted, indignant. I'm not sure Talia heard me over her helpless, relieved laughter. It was infectious, and before

I knew it I was laughing too. And then I realized she was still crying, and that I had started crying, and we held each other and laughed and cried until we were both out of breath.

"You're not hurt, are you?" Talia asked. "Sorry, I didn't mean to knock you over like that, I was just... so excited, y'know?" She rolled off me, getting to her feet and offering me a hand. I took it.

"It's fine. I think I did more damage to the ground than the ground did to me." I stood up, dusting off the back of my skirt. "A little dirt never killed anyone."

"But your dress is so nice, and it's *Shabbat...*" Talia looked a bit fretful.

I rested a hand on her shoulder. "It's *fine,*" I repeated. "Nobody's going to notice a little dirt on my butt." I gave her a once-over. "How are you feeling? You seemed really stressed out."

"I think I'll be okay," Talia assured me. "I was *really* stressing over telling you, but now that I have, I feel a lot better." She glanced at me once, then looked away, fidgeting a bit with her skirt.

"Something else on your mind?"

"Well... er, no, I think I've put enough on you for one night." I looked a bit closer, and to my surprise, Talia was blushing. Not out of nervousness like before, but... well, it seemed she was blushing out of *embarrassment.*

Now I had a hunch.

"Hmm," I responded. I reached out to take her hand, and watched as she flushed even darker. "What if I can read your mind?"

Talia snorted. "You totally can't."

"Wanna bet? I bet I can tell you what you're thinking right now."

Talia rolled her eyes. "You sooooooo cannot."

I pressed two fingers to my temple. "I'm getting something… yes, it's a question! A question that's been burning in your mind since you invited me out here… it's coming to me…"

"Reina—" Talia started.

"You're thinking, 'I wonder if Reina has a crush on me too!'"

Talia froze. Her blush spread down her neck to her shoulders, and she looked a bit like a deer caught in headlights. I grinned, ignoring my heart threatening to jackhammer its way out of my ribcage.

"W-well," Talia spluttered, "th-that's—um—I didn't tell you *just* because I—" She sighed. "Okay. Fine. I like you. Happy?"

Good thing I was right. "Very happy!" I replied. I reached down and took her hand. Talia twitched in surprise. "After all," I continued, "my crush has been pretty unbearable the last couple weeks too. This cute girl just *had* to be completely charming and fun to talk to."

Talia stared at me. "Wait," she said slowly, "so you—"

"Uh-huh."

"And I—"

"Yup."

"So maybe we—"

"We sure could."

Talia's mouth flapped open and shut as she tried to comprehend what exactly had just happened. Before she could figure out what to say next, though, we were interrupted by a loud "HEY!"

We both turned, startled, to see a lifeguard coming up the hill, frowning at us. "You aren't supposed to be here right now!" he barked. "Services are starting soon. Get back to your cabins, both of you!" He made a shooing gesture, and the two of us scrambled back toward the path, laughing breathlessly.

"Hey," I said. "We still have a little longer before services start. And nobody's out except us." I paused. "Out of their cabins, I mean." Talia laughed a bit. "You want to, uh... go on another walk?"

Talia smiled warmly at me, and it was different this time—warmer, more adoring. She took my hand, interlacing our fingers together, and squeezed gently. "Yeah," she said. "I'd like that."

It didn't take us long to do another lap around the bunks, but it was close enough to sundown that we headed to the shul early. Shul was really just a clearing in a grove of trees by the dining hall, but I liked it even better than the sanctuary at my shul back at home. When everyone was around, singing the prayers I was slowly learning, it truly felt holy.

Chaverim bunk's section was toward the back, so we settled on the benches and waited, watching the clouds in the sky turn purple as the sun slipped past the horizon. A breeze rippled the grass and fluttered our skirts. Talia shivered, and I only hesitated for a moment before wrapping an arm around her shoulders. She turned to face me, smiling, and leaned in close. I didn't realize what she was aiming for until her lips began to purse, and I flinched, leaving her to land a kiss on my cheek instead of where she was aiming.

Talia giggled. "Sorry, did I scare you?"

I flushed. "No!" I hissed, though she had definitely surprised me. "It's just—you know, I kinda suck at like, all things? And I saw you coming and my brain slammed a fist on that fight-or-flight button and I *guess* it picked flight because what would fight have even been—wow, that analogy makes no sense. I'm talking too much. Do you think I'm talking too much? You can tell me to shut up if I'm talking too much, or I might just chatter forever and—"

Talia caught my chin between her finger and thumb, and my voice died in my throat as she gave me an amused smile.

"You talk too much," she said, looking around to be sure no one could see us. We were all alone. And then she kissed me.

For a short, glorious moment, there was nobody in the world but us, hand in hand, sharing the same breath. My entire body felt so light I could float away. It could never have lasted long enough, but it was cut far too short as the sound of cabin doors opening in the distance reached us. We pulled apart as though we'd been burned, and I felt my face flush to a new shade of red.

Talia glanced at me and laughed a little. "You got a little…" She dabbed at her lips a bit, and I mimicked her gesture, looking at the red lipstick smeared on my fingertips and probably the rest of my mouth.

"Oh, yeah," I said weakly. "That's a problem."

"Run inside the mess hall bathroom and clean up," she said. "I'll cover you."

"Thanks."

Five minutes later, I was back in my seat, lipstick-free and reciting the evening prayers along with everyone else. My heart was beating so hard I was sure Talia next to me could hear it—I kissed a girl! I kissed a girl *right in the middle of camp!* I'd only kissed a girl one other time, and it was more like a brief peck than a *real* kiss. I was still dizzy just thinking about it.

If this is a dream, I thought, *I don't want to wake up.*

After Shabbat morning prayers I took a nap with Talia in her bed. It was the first time I had slept in the same bed as another person, sharing warmth beneath the sheets, curling into each other's bodies. We fell asleep with hands intertwined, and had Rachel not shaken us awake, we would have been late for lunch. We made it on time and held hands beneath the table as we ate. I couldn't help but bask in how happy I was; in fact, I couldn't remember the last time I felt this happy.

Discussion groups were held in each bunk on Saturday afternoons, so an hour later I found myself part of a circle made up of Chaverim Bunk Four. A few of the girls chatted, finishing up conversations that had started during lunch, but the conversations smothered themselves as Rachel and Sarah sat down as well.

"Alright ladies," Sarah said, "discussion today is gonna be a bit serious, and it's going to involve some topics that not everyone here may fully understand or be familiar with. Don't be afraid to ask questions, but don't jump down anyone's throat if they say something you think is inconsiderate either. Take the opportunity to teach them. Everyone got it?" She looked around the circle, taking in the bobbing heads, and continued.

"Rachel and I want to talk to you about some policy changes at the camp, specifically policies regarding LGBTQ campers."

My heart jumped in my throat. Did Sarah suspect something because she saw Talia and me napping together? Did she see Talia kiss me the night before? Did she catch me looking at a girl too long? I glanced around the circle, but the rest of the campers had their eyes glued on Sarah, who was still talking.

"We're probably going to mention a few terms not everyone is going to know, so if you're confused on anything, just raise a hand and we'll hash out a definition."

We're going to talk about the gay community. In other words, I was about to learn exactly what my bunkmates and counselors thought of people like me. Talia and I shared a glance; she looked calm, and I probably did too, but there was no way either of us could be calm in this situation.

"The camp's current stance," Sarah went on, "is that it stands under the Conservative movement, which follows many old practices that are interpreted in a different light by other movements. This, and by extension the camp, is not inherently homophobic." I rolled my eyes and regretted it at once, but fortunately nobody seemed to notice. "But as things have been changing in America, the camp has decided to reexamine some of its policies. The good news is that that invites growth and change. The bad news is not everyone agrees and some want to keep the camp's 'traditional' values, even if it means alienating some campers."

"All this is to say," Rachel added, "that the camp is considering changing its policy regarding openly gay campers and staff."

I raised my hand, and Sarah nodded at me. "I don't remember reading anything about these policies on the website, so what are the current policies? Are they official policies, or just unofficial practices?"

"Great questions," Sarah said. "There are official policies in place, but they only really come up on a need-to-know basis, so they aren't publicly available anywhere." She paused for a moment. "To my understanding, the policy is that anyone who comes out, camper or staff member, is sent home, and can't return in the future. And kids who get kicked out get outed to their parents, which can obviously be super harmful. The rationale behind the policy is it's supposed to make campers and their parents feel safe, but… well, can anyone see the problem with this?"

"Safe?" Talia scoffed. "Safe from what? Do they think it's a disease or something? Like they're afraid that little Joshy is gonna catch the gay?"

For a moment I was afraid she was going to say something about us, and my heart started beating loudly and faster. I held my breath for a minute, but when she didn't say anything like that, I calmed down.

"Well there's a fear, which is completely unfounded, that gay people are predatory," Sarah said. She looked down at the floor when she said it as if she didn't want us to see her face turn red with anger, shame, embarrassment, or some mix of the three.

"It's an old stupid lie, but some people believe it," Rachel added.

"First off, that's bullshit and so gross," Hadassah snapped. "And I understand the camp is trying to make everyone feel safe, but doesn't it do the opposite for anyone who's gay? The policy would make them feel unsafe here. Even targeted." She frowned deeply.

"This whole thing feels like bullying to me," Shelly said. "And it doesn't seem right to exclude people who came here to enjoy themselves."

"Good interpretation," said Sarah. "That's how a lot of parents are looking at the matter, which is why there's a debate over whether to change the rules. Rachel and I thought it would be important to bring campers into the conversation, too. It's important that everyone at this camp feels safe and respected, and we want to find a way to make that happen in this bunk and in the rest of the camp. How do you think this matter should be resolved? Should the policy stay, and risk alienating future campers? Or should it change, and risk some people taking their kids out of camp?"

The room was silent for a moment as we considered what Sarah had said. Was it better for the camp to keep the policy, or to change it and make campers like me and Talia feel safer?

Talia broke the silence a second before it got too uncomfortable. "Who's calling for the change? Is it parents, or former campers, or staff members?"

"It's the new assistant director, actually," Rachel said. "He's been pushing for the change as soon as he took the job. He isn't gay himself, so he isn't directly impacted by the situation, but he still feels compelled to change it. He thinks the current policies for LGBTQ campers are draconic, so he's fighting to change them."

Sasha raised her hand next. "What do all those letters stand for?" she asked. "I think I know all of them except the Q."

I jumped in before Sarah or Rachel could answer. "It stands for lesbian, gay, bisexual, and transgender," I said. "The Q can stand for either questioning, which is for someone who doesn't know how to identify yet, or queer, which can be used as a big umbrella term for all of the above."

"Wait," Tova said. "How does the policy affect transgender people? I thought it was just about if you came out as gay."

"Gender identity is a big part of the discussion," Rachel said, "especially since the camp separates bunks based on gender. The camp board thinks that someone is going to be uncomfortable whether campers are assigned to bunks based on their gender identity or the gender they were assigned at birth, so neither option is on the table. There's a lot of talk going on to find a way all campers feel comfortable and respected, but it isn't easy."

"There are also nonbinary people," Tova said. "Would they get to choose their bunk?"

"That's another question," Sarah said. "There's a lot the camp is trying to figure out.

Rachel fiddled with a bracelet on her wrist. "Jews have been persecuted and abused since the beginning of history," she said. "Egypt and the Pharaoh, Russia and the Czar, the Spanish Inquisition, the Holocaust—even today, we're targeted by the alt-right and even some mainstream politicians." She looked up at all of us. "Why is that? I mean, *really*, why is that? It's a question that everyone in this room, at this *camp*, should ask themselves before passing judgment on anyone else, especially among our own tribe. Discrimination for any reason is wrong.

It happens every day, all over the world, and we're trying to keep some of that out of the camp."

"Rachel—" Sarah began, but Rachel stopped her.

"It's fine," she said. "You guys can probably tell I'm more than a little invested in this issue." She took a deep breath. "My sister, Jane, was a camper here for many years. In the middle of the summer, she came out to her bunkmates as a lesbian, and the camp made her leave." Rachel smiled at the floor, but it was bitter. "She felt safe enough at Camp Geshem to do something she couldn't do anywhere else. Not at home. Not at school. Not in our hometown. *Here.* She felt safe enough *here* to be her full, authentic self, because this place was like home to her. And the camp… had a problem with that."

Tears had begun to bead in the corner of Rachel's eyes as she talked, and Sarah put an arm around her. "She was heartbroken," she went on. "Her camp family couldn't accept who she was and pushed her away. They even made her out her girlfriend, who got sent home too. That bitterness and rejection built up inside her, and she started…" Rachel paused. "…making bad decisions. Let's put it that way. She's alright now, thank God for therapy, but she wasn't for a while."

I couldn't help but wonder what she meant by bad decisions. I couldn't help but wonder how her sister felt, being rejected because of who she was and who she loved. Was I going to end up like that?

Rachel was still talking. "It was scary," she said, "watching her self-destruct like that, and all because of camp. Things changed between her and my parents when her counselor outed her. It's still rocky honestly. It really messed her up." She wiped her eyes with the heel of her hand. "I—I don't want to see that happen to anyone else. This place is so important to—to so many people. I don't want this camp, and the people you meet here, to become a painful memory. I don't want *this place* to be the reason you want to hurt yourself or—or anyone else." She was crying harder now, wiping her face on a piece of cloth Sarah offered her. "I'm really proud of you all for understanding this issue so well. It's so good to see that after what Jane went through. My sister would be proud of you all."

Sarah looked out at the circle of fidgeting girls, all wearing worried expressions. "Alright, alright," she said. "Group hug."

Almost as one, Chaverim Bunk Four surged forward and piled onto each other with Rachel, now laughing through her tears, in the middle. In the middle of the tangle of limbs, I managed to find Talia, and we hugged tightly.

"Those rules," she whispered, "those rules are changing for us. Those stupid, dumb, awful, outdated dinosaur rules."

Chapter Four

Life went on. Chaverim Four was easier to get along with than I thought—and so was hiding my relationship with Talia. Most of the girls around the camp were physically affectionate with each other, and handholding, snuggling, and even cheek kisses were well within the norm. It was easy to stay under the radar, which was a necessity in Camp Geshem; the same rules that had exiled Rachel's sister threatened us now, and even being able to pass off romantic gestures as platonic wasn't enough to make us feel at ease. Keeping our guard up was exhausting, even if we weren't as afraid.

The reality of the situation hammered itself in again one day as we were walking back to our bunk before dinner. Talia was detailing her eventful arts and crafts session that had ended with the teacher lunging for the fire extinguisher. Talia was chattering animatedly, gesturing with the hand I wasn't holding. I loved how her eyes sparkled when she got excited about something. We were just about to turn toward the cabin when a voice sounded out behind us, calling, "Talia!"

Talia looked surprised for the briefest second before ripping her hand out of mine and spinning on her heel toward the voice. I blinked and scanned her face for a reason—girls holding hands wasn't uncommon here—but she didn't even look at me.

"Naomi!" she said, tone bubbly. "I didn't know you were working this year."

The approaching girl wore a staff shirt and looked about college-aged, like our own counselors. "You think I'd pass up a summer at Geshem?" she grinned. "Dream on, shortstuff."

Talia smiled. "Oh. Naomi, this is Reina. We're in the same bunk this year. Reina, this is Naomi. She's friends with my older sister."

"Nice to meet you," I said politely.

"Good to see Talia's making friends," Naomi said. "Keep an eye on her and make sure she doesn't cause trouble, alright Reina?"

"I'll do my best."

Talia and Naomi chatted a bit longer, but I wasn't really listening to any of it. I couldn't stop thinking about how quickly Talia had pulled her hand from mine. Was she that worried about being found out? Or was there another, uglier reason? I knew I needed to trust Talia, but the insecurities circling my mind refused to go anywhere.

"Oh shoot," Naomi said, checking her watch. "I gotta run or I'll be late. See you two later!" She said her goodbyes and raced toward one of the administrative buildings in the center of the campgrounds.

Talia watched her go, and it was only when the door had closed behind Naomi, when the reminder of her family was gone, that she reached out and took my hand again. "Jeez, what a chatterbox," she said, grinning. "She always stops and makes conversation when she doesn't have time. Makes her late to everything."

"Seems like it," I agreed, but I wasn't really listening.

Talia looked at me. "Okay," she said. "What's up?"

"Nothing's up."

"You're a bad liar, Reina." She pulled on my hand. "C'mon, talk to me."

While I hadn't known her for long, I'd learned one important thing about Talia: she never stopped until she got the answer she was looking for. And this was one of those things that would simmer and rot in my gut otherwise, so it was better if I talked to her about it now.

"It's just… you let go of my hand when Naomi came," I said, piecing my words together. "And it's not like I'm mad or anything, it's just that it felt… I don't know. Like you were ashamed or embarrassed of me. Never mind, it's stupid," I said quickly, seeing her face drain of color. "I'm probably just overthinking things, you don't have to worry about it, I'm fine—"

I cut myself off as Talia pulled me into a hug. She held me tightly, burying her face in my shoulder, and it took me a minute to register she was trembling. "It's not that," she said, voice small. "I'm not ashamed or embarrassed of you, I promise. Do you remember how I told you my being pansexual was a secret you couldn't tell anyone?"

My stomach tightened. I knew where this was going. "I do."

Talia pulled away from me, and although she wasn't crying, she wiped at her eyes with the heel of her hand and stared at the ground. Her shoulders were slumped over and she seemed so small. "My family doesn't know," she confessed. "Nobody does. Not my friends, not my parents, not my brother or sister or anyone. I only told you what I am because I thought you might be too, and I didn't want to be alone anymore. But it's awful—it's like I'm guilty for being myself, because that 'self' isn't what people expect me to be."

I nodded. "Like you're going to let everyone down by existing."

"Exactly," she said. "It's like I have to keep the biggest part of me a secret. And I know that you're out at home, and I know that had to have taken a lot of courage, but…" She wasn't looking me in the eye. "I can't do that. And I'm afraid of pulling you back into the closet with me. I don't want to make you go through all that again."

"Talia," I said firmly. "I don't mind."

Talia looked up at me, eyes watery. "What? But—"

"Whatever works for you," I interrupted, "is whatever works for both of us—that's fine. If you can't be out, then I won't say anything. If you decide to come out, I'll be next to you. We're in this together. I promise."

Talia's lip quivered, and she wiped at her face again. "Oh, Reina," she whispered, "how did I get so lucky to meet you?"

The next morning, I was woken up with a hug. When I pried my eyes open, I could see that Rachel was moving on to the next bunk and hugging Tova. I sat up and stared, seeing Sarah doing the same to the bunks on the other side of the cabin.

"What's going on?" I asked Amanda, who'd been awoken before me. She only shrugged.

"It's a very special day," Rachel hummed, standing beside Irene as she rubbed the sleep from her eyes. "Does anyone know what day it is?"

I looked at my watch. "Uh, July 15th...?"

"Close, but no!" Sarah said. "I'll give you a hint: we're halfway through the Hebrew month of Av." She looked around the cabin, evidently disappointed with the number of blank stares she received from girls who did not bother to keep track of the Hebrew calendar. "Oh, come on, what are they teaching in religious school these days?" she huffed.

"It's Tu B'Av!" Shelly shouted, and she jumped from her bed like she was propelled by a rocket. "Everyone wake up, it's Tu B'Av!"

"Sorry," Talia yawned, "but my brain is only like, half working. What's Tu B'Av again?"

"You can think of it like Valentine's Day," Shelly explained.

"It got picked up again in the last few decades, but it was an important date thousands of years ago. It used to be a holiday for unmarried women to find suitors. They'd dress up in white and go to the center of the village, where the village men would walk around and pick their bride. Isn't that cute?"

I couldn't help it; I snorted in disgust. "Sounds like a nightmare to me," I said. "Could you imagine a total stranger grabbing you in the town square and being like, 'Hey, you're hot. Let's get hitched in that parking lot over there.'"

A few girls laughed, but Shelly's face screwed up in annoyance. "Actually, back when that was a normal custom, Jewish villages were really small so everyone would know each other. I'd rather get married that way than through some arranged marriage with a guy older than my dad like they did elsewhere."

"Alright girls," interrupted Rachel, "let's step back a bit. The origins of the holiday aren't that important, and everyone's entitled to their own opinions. We're going to celebrate today like they celebrate in Israel, with hearts and candy and everything else. Sound good?"

The cabin murmured its consent, and the girls who were still in bed got out to get dressed for the day. I wasn't sure how I felt about how the holiday started, but it was a holiday about love, and I was excited to celebrate it with Talia. *But before I do that,* I thought, glancing toward Shelly, *there's something else I need to do.*

I approached Shelly after we had both gotten dressed. She was still pouting a bit, but she didn't turn away when she saw me.

"Hey," I said. "I'm, uh, sorry I was rude about Tu B'Av. It seems like a lot of fun, really. I'm just not crazy about the whole… arranged marriage thing, y'know?"

Shelly rolled her eyes. "Whatever. You don't have to get all sour about love and stuff just because you don't have your eye on someone."

I blinked, and my heart started to thud in my chest. "What do you mean?"

"We've all noticed," Shelly said, waving in the general direction of the rest of the cabin. My mouth went dry and I shoved my hands in my shorts to hide how sweaty they suddenly were. "You always get all quiet when the rest of us talk about crushes or boyfriends. It's pretty obvious you don't have anyone you like right now, so I guess I can see why you'd be bitter about a holiday like Tu B'Av."

Oh, that's what she meant. My heart slowed to a normal pace, and Shelly kept going. "I guess I shouldn't have snapped at you either," she said. "I get cranky in the mornings, plus being reminded about Tu B'Av made me miss Israel a little, y'know?" I figured the best response would be just to nod, so that's what I did. "Thanks for understanding," she said, and finally smiled.

"Are we cool?" I asked.

"Yeah, we're cool, Reina," she said. "You wanna hug it out?"

She spread her arms, and I went in for the hug. I caught sight of Talia over her shoulder; she was grinning. Behind her, Rachel clapped her hands to get our attention. "We're not doing the usual today," she announced. "When you're all dressed, come to the center of the bunk and we'll have some fun."

Ten minutes later, we assembled as instructed. Sarah had started playing a playlist of love songs, and Rachel had retrieved a cardboard box covered with a pink beach towel. She passed around the treasure inside: pink-frosted cupcakes, fixings for cereal, plastic bowls, and…

"Fruit!" Sasha shouted. "I haven't seen fruit since we got here!" She pulled packages of strawberries, cherries, and raspberries from the box.

Irene said, "Sasha, dial it back a bit. It's too early. Besides, we're all excited about the fruit."

"But there's fruit in the dining hall all the time," Hadassah pointed out.

"You're absolutely right, Hadassah," Talia said. "We have our choice of fruit from the dining hall. Would you like a squishy apple, overripe banana, or a rock-hard peach?"

The bunk laughed, but Sarah said, "Girls, we should be thankful for… oh, who am I kidding, the fruit here sucks. I was going to say we should be thankful for what we have, and we should, but that doesn't mean we can never complain."

"I found a worm in an apple the third day of camp," I chimed in. "I haven't eaten a piece of fruit since. It's a miracle I haven't gotten scurvy."

"Someone pass Reina the fruit before she keels over," Sarah said among the cabin's laughter. She produced pink paper plates and plastic cutlery from the box and passed it around the circle after the fruit.

"What's scurvy?" Tova asked. "You aren't sick, are you Reina?" She looked genuinely worried, and I couldn't tell if she was joking or not.

"Tova, I love you with all my heart," Amanda said, "but you really aren't the sharpest knife in the drawer, are you?"

"What about a knife?" Tova asked, confused.

"She's calling you stupid," Talia translated.

"Oh," Tova said. "But what's scurvy?"

Rachel and Sarah launched into a simplified explanation while the rest of us dug into the fruit and cupcakes. Hadassah passed me the strawberries, and they tasted sweeter than anything I'd had in weeks.

"By the way," Talia said, "we're all comparing Tu B'Av to Valentine's Day, but does anyone know the history behind Valentine's?" Without waiting for anyone to reply, she continued. "It started in the 5th century—"

"As all good stories must," Sasha interrupted. Giggles rolled around the cabin.

"And for some reason, the Romans had decided marriage was illegal. I don't really know why, but that's not important," Talia went on. "What *is* important is that a man named Valentine decided to officiate marriages, even on penalty of death. And of course, the Romans found out and... I think they crucified him?" She shrugged. "Romans liked doing that. The date he died was February 14th, and thus a Hallmark holiday was born." She gave a theatrical bow as we all clapped.

"The history behind some of our holidays isn't always pretty," Rachel said, "but what's important is how we celebrate them now. Though I *will* admit that the old Tu B'Av traditions appeal to me more than arranged marriages. The idea of marrying a total stranger has always creeped me out. I mean, can you imagine?" She looked around the circle. "Not meeting the man you're going to marry until your wedding day? Could you imagine walking down the aisle without knowing who's going to be greeting you at the end? Without knowing if he'll be kind or cruel? It must be terrifying."

"It still happens in some countries," Irene said. "It doesn't mean the people are unhappy, because to them it's the way things have always been. And a lot of the time the marriages work out. I mean, they had to work out in the old days, or else a lot of us probably wouldn't be here."

"I took a class on old-world traditions last year," Sarah said. "We had a unit on arranged marriage, and the idea always made me mad. My grandparents were in an arranged marriage, and they weren't happy about it. They became friends over time, and raised their kids, but when I asked my grandma about it she said they had never loved each other." She frowned. "They never divorced—too traditionalist for that—but the idea of living your life with someone you don't even love always made me sad."

"It's always bothered me when someone has a say in someone else's marriage," said Talia. "But more than anything else, I've always hated how it's seen as such a sacred institution that it needs legal protection. There are so many hoops you have to jump through in some places. Like in other countries where you can't even marry someone the same gender as you!"

Uh-oh. I tried to catch Talia's eye to indicate to her she should stop, but she kept going, working herself up more as she talked.

"You know who you can marry where I live?" she said. "Your first cousin. Someone that shares a quarter of your DNA. You can marry your own *family*. But two girls marrying is out of the question for no good reason! That's just absurd to me."

"Hear! Hear!" Rachel cheered. "Looks like we've got a future politician here, huh?"

Talia shook her head. "Politicians only do what's popular with their base," she said. "If they don't appeal to their voters, they can't keep their job, so they don't enact any real change. Just because something is popular doesn't mean it's right. I'm planning on going to law school to be a civil rights lawyer, so I can fight for people the law overlooks." She stopped and glanced around the room, apparently only now registering that the entire bunk was watching her. Her cheeks flushed in embarrassment.

"I stand corrected, then," Rachel said. "Looks like we have a future lawyer in our midst."

Most of the bunk laughed, but I stared at Talia. She had thought about her future way more than I had. I wasn't even thinking about what I would do once I left high school, and here she was with the next ten years of her life planned out. Not even some adults could think that far ahead. Talia was amazing.

The rest of the day was filled with more holiday-themed activities that Rachel produced from a seemingly endless number of boxes. We had very stale candy hearts which I figured were left over from Valentine's Day, and they gave us all little stuffed animals. They were the cheap kind that you win in a claw machine, but I was still happy when I got handed the only unicorn in the group. I had more fun than I had expected, and before I knew it, the sun had set, we'd eaten dinner, and our counselors were leading us to a bonfire pit. Sarah worked on lighting the fire while Rachel produced yet another cardboard box. I had no idea where she was keeping them.

"Congratulations!" she announced as we sat down. The fire flared to life behind her. "And welcome to your wedding!"

We stared at her.

"You heard me," Rachel said, and she held up the box. "You'll take a name from the box, and propose to whoever you get, then that person picks a name, and so on. Sound good?" We all nodded, and Rachel grinned. "Great! Then let's get started!"

Sarah stood up behind Rachel, dusting her hands off. "I'll kick us off by proposing to Rachel so you have an idea of what to say." She circled the bonfire, looked at Rachel, and dropped to one knee. Rachel mock-gasped and clapped her hands to her cheeks.

"Rachel," Sarah declared, one hand outstretched, the other on her chest, "we've been best friends since we were ten, and shared a bunk every year we came to Geshem. I was so excited when I found out we would be counselors in the same bunk. My love for you knows no bounds, so I ask you, from the bottom of my heart, will you marry me?" She produced what was obviously a cheap plastic ring, but Rachel reacted as if it was the real deal.

"Oh, Sarah," she gushed, "yes, yes, a million times yes!" She slid the ring on her finger, helped Sarah up, and the two hugged to the sounds of our cheers. They released each other and Rachel looked at us. "Got the idea? Who wants to start us off?"

Tova raised her hand, and Rachel held out the box for her. Tova rummaged in the box for a few seconds before pulling a piece of paper out. She unfolded it, squinted in the darkness, turned it upside down, and then looked up. "Hadassah, I got you."

Hadassah stood up to scattered applause and stood before the bonfire, just as Rachel had a minute ago. Sarah handed Tova another plastic ring, and Tova got down on one knee.

"Hadassah," she began, "I love you like a sister. A sister I only started getting along with this summer." This drew a few laughs from the bunk.

Talia leaned over to me and whispered, "Those two used to fight all the time over any old thing. I swear, once they argued about the lunch line order." I snickered.

Tova was continuing. "I'm glad that we started getting along this year. I don't know what changed, but it's been a great summer so far. Even when I couldn't stand you, I cared for you to the bottom of my heart. I hope we can always stay friends." With that heartfelt ending, Tova stood and slid the ring on Hadassah's finger.

As Tova straightened, Hadassah pulled her into an embrace. "I'm glad we stopped fighting too," she said. "We're pretty good friends when we aren't screaming our heads off at each other." They laughed and Tova sat back down, leaving Hadassah to pick out the next name.

Her face lit up. "Talia!"

Talia next to me stood up and joined Hadassah in front of the fire, and I tried to ignore the twinge of jealousy in my stomach. Even though I knew it was silly, I wanted to propose to Talia too. Why did Hadassah get to do it?

"Talia, what is there to say?" Hadassah started. "I've known you for forever. We were side by side in the nursery ward, in preschool, and in the synagogue. If it weren't for the fact we're in separate school districts, we'd spend all our days side by side. Fortunately, here at camp, we can make that dream a reality. Will you continue on this journey at my side and marry me and also this bunk?"

"Yes, of course I will!" Talia gushed. Was it just the light of the bonfire, or was she actually blushing that hard? "I can't believe you started that far back, jeez."

"What can I say? I'm a hopeless romantic," Hadassah replied, shrugging. She sat down next to Tova as Talia pulled out the next name. A massive smile curled on her face.

"Reina," she said.

I'd been hoping she would have called my name, but now that she had, it didn't feel real. Still, I stood and crossed the distance to the fire pit, standing before her. Talia dropped to one knee, and that was enough to make me flush and smile, out of both excitement and embarrassment. "Reina," she said, taking one of my hands in both of hers. "I never imagined I would find my other half at this camp. You are the yin to my yang, the laces to my sneakers, the pineapple to my pizza."

I laughed. "You like pineapple on pizza? Uh-oh, Talia, I don't know if this is going to work out."

"Aww, c'mon, let's not make that of all things the dealbreaker," Talia said, winking. The rest of the bunk laughed, which helped flush some of the anxiety out of my stomach. "I'm glad we met—in fact, I can't believe we've only known each other for three and a half weeks. I never understood the phrase 'where have you been all my life' until I met you. You make my world a brighter place, and I'm so happy I have a chance to be with you." She slid the platic ring on my finger, and as she stood, she brushed a tear from my cheek I hadn't even realized had fallen. I pulled her into a hug, and she whispered, just for me to hear, "I mean every word."

I knew. I knew she meant it. I could hear it in her voice, see it in her eyes. She meant everything she said in a way the rest of the bunk could never understand.

Rachel's voice pierced through my hazy fog of happiness. "Now say, 'will you marry this bunk?'" she called.

"Oh, right," Talia said, pulling away. "Will you marry this bunk?"

I grinned and kissed her cheek. "Oh, Talia," I said. "Yes."

Chapter Five

"Clean, clean, clean!" Rachel shouted. "Clean like there's no tomorrow!"

"Guys, if you want to have fun tonight, you'd better make this bunk spic-and-span," warned Sarah. She consulted her watch. "It's nine-thirty now. If we don't stop cleaning we can get approved by ten, and then we can party til midnight. C'mon, this is your last night to party!"

"What? No it's not," Sasha said. "Chaverim Three is leaving tomorrow, not us. We're here for the whole summer, not half. Why do *we* have to clean?"

"Because, girls," Sarah said, "your parents are going to be here tomorrow. If your rooms at home were in this condition, would they let you do anything other than clean your room? I know mine wouldn't. Besides, Rachel and I are supposed to be helping you become self-sufficient so you can live on your own, and living on your own means cleaning up after yourself."

"She's got a point, guys," Talia said. "I mean, do you see this place? Total disaster zone." She gestured to the stray socks and underwear scattered around the bunk floor, the sticky patch of orange soda by the garbage can, and the funky-smelling towel that was *somewhere* in the carnage. I didn't even want to think about how bad the bathroom was. The bunk laughed as though seeing the mess for the first time, even though we'd all been living in it.

"There's more to it than that," said Rachel. "A dirty living space can stress you out even if you don't notice it. Getting rid of the mess can clear your head and give you some breathing room, both figuratively and literally. So let's spruce up the place... but if they ask, how it looks tomorrow is exactly as clean as it's been all summer, alright?" We nodded and laughed.

"This is exactly as clean as it's been all summer," Rosie said. "And our counselors never swear. Especially not in front of us." The counselors looked a little bit embarrassed, but neither of them could say they had abstained from swearing in front of the campers. They had explained it earlier in the summer: we wouldn't get in trouble for swearing as long as we didn't tell the directors that the counselors were swearing. As long as everyone was fine with it, it worked.

As I swept, I reflected on the past four weeks. When I first got here, my parents told me to have fun, and I didn't think I'd be able to. Now I couldn't believe that I had once been so hesitant to come here. I couldn't believe how lucky I was. Camp Geshem was infamous for being unsafe for LGBTQ campers, yet somehow I'd found someone else like me, and had even started a relationship.

An arm wrapped around my waist; Talia stood there, hefting a garbage bag in her free hand. "Hey, help me with the garbage, would you?"

She led me from the bunk and we started toward the nearby dumpster. It was dark and quiet; we had already done Havdalah, so it was late in the evening. There were more stars than I could count, and no one around but us.

She pulled me in close to her, her face only inches from mine. She whispered in my ear, "So my parents are coming tomorrow."

I laughed and whispered back, "Yeah, and my parents are also coming. Everyone's parents are coming. That's kind of the point of Parent Day."

"I think that I want to introduce you to them."

My pulse quickened. I knew meeting your partner's parents was supposed to be nerve-wracking, but I hadn't realized just *how* nerve-wracking. My mind raced with thoughts I didn't know how to put into words. Talia seemed to notice how overwhelmed I suddenly was, because she stopped walking and I did too.

"You want me to meet your parents?" I asked, just to clarify. She nodded. "And when you say you want me to meet your parents... do you want them to meet your new friend Reina, or your new girlfriend? I... are you telling me you're going to come out to them?"

Talia froze. "Ah," she said weakly. "I didn't actually... think that far. Maybe I should've put more thought into this."

I laughed. "Yeah, you think? Did you just forget you're closeted?"

"Don't make fun of me," Talia whined. "I got so excited thinking about introducing you to them I didn't think about anything else."

"Good thing you decided to talk about it with me then," I said, amused. "You should try to figure out beforehand what you're going to say. Are you going to tell them that you identify as pan? And are you going to tell them that you're seeing someone? That that someone is me, or even just someone at camp? I mean, I don't want to pressure you. You shouldn't feel like you need to come out to your parents because of me, especially if you haven't put a ton of thought into it."

"I'm not doing this for you," she said matter-of-factly. "I'm doing this for me. I'm pansexual, and I want my parents to know. It wouldn't be important, except for that I'm dating you, so... you know, I should probably mention you in all of this, right? I don't know, what do you think?"

"I don't know," I finally said. "I mean, it's different for everyone. Have you thought about what they're going to say? What you're going to say is roughly half of it, but I'm sure that they're going to have some questions. I mean, mine did, even though they were totally fine with it. Do you know how they're going to react? Or do you at least have any idea?"

As I looked at her, the color slowly drained from Talia's face. The dumpster was right there, but she dropped the garbage bag and sat down on the ground, holding her head in her hands. "Oh my god," she whispered. "I haven't thought this through at all. What am I doing?"

I sat next to her and wrapped an arm around her shoulders, pulled her in close to me. She buried her head in my shoulder and muffled a groan into it. I ran my fingers through her hair, trying to be soothing. "You'll be fine," I murmured. "I'll help you through this." I felt a little responsible; would she be considering coming out to her parents if she hadn't met me?

Talia lifted her head to look at me, tears in her eyes. She looked so frightened, so lost. She reminded me of myself when I came out to my parents. Deep down, I think I knew they would have been fine with it, and they had been. But I didn't know if the same was true for Talia and her parents. Would she be this afraid to come out to them if they were?

"You'll be fine," I repeated. "It'll work out, I promise. If you don't tell your parents tomorrow, you can tell them the day after that, or the day after that. You can tell them when you get back from camp, or whenever you want, as long as you're comfortable. You don't have to tell them right away, though trust me, I get the urge. But you should make a plan. You need to figure out what you're going to say, how you're going to handle their reactions, and a plan for what comes after, whatever that looks like."

She nodded, still looking unsure of herself. "How do I know what they're going to do? I mean, how are they going to react?" That was a good question, and one that maybe just about every queer teen wanted an answer to at some point. Human reactions were such a tricky thing.

I said, "There really isn't a surefire way to figure out how they're going to react. There are some people who support queer rights in theory but react differently when it comes to their own family, because it affects them personally."

"Wait," Talia said. "If they support all of those things, then why would they not be okay if their own kid came out?"

"There aren't any real reasons, if you ask me," I told her. "Just ugly excuses. People try to make up excuses to validate their homophobia. It's all bigotry, plain and simple. One of my favorite teachers at school got really weird and uncomfortable around me after I came out to her and she never said why. She'd embarrass me in front of the whole class for no reason, that sort of thing. My mom thought maybe she resented me because she wasn't out, or something like that. You never know."

"She sounds like a tool," Talia sniffed.

"You're right," I agreed. "But anyway, some people will say things like, 'Why would you choose to be like this? Did we do something wrong? Are you punishing us? How do you know? Does this mean that you're having sex? This means that you can never have children.' Stuff like that. I'm sure that you've heard things like that before."

Talia tilted her head. "I mean, I've read about that kind of stuff online," she said, "but I've never met someone who's experienced that. I don't even know what I would do if my parents asked me any of those things, or said anything like that to me. What did you tell your parents? How did they react? Did they take it well?"

I chuckled. "It's kind of a funny story," I said. "Well. I didn't think it was funny, but my mom did. See, I'd been questioning my sexuality for over a year by that point. I knew I liked girls, but I wasn't sure if I still liked boys. I hadn't been attracted to any recently, but I remembered having crushes on some when

I was younger. So I decided I'd come out as bi, because I was worried if I came out as a lesbian and then got a crush on a boy people wouldn't take me seriously or they'd call me confused.

"I decided to tell my mom first. I thought of everything. I prepared this whole speech, came up with responses to every possible argument, practiced in my mirror for days. Then I finally told her one night. I said, 'Mom, I think I'm bisexual.' And you know what she said to me? She said, 'Reina, darling, you're a lesbian. Your father and I have known for years. What took you so long, honey?'"

Talia burst out laughing. The sound made me warm and fuzzy. "Oh my god," she wheezed. "That's just... actually, I don't know what that is."

"It sure was something," I agreed. "I mean, it went better than I thought it would. I'm lucky my family was so cool about it. You have to remember that your parents are people too, and you can't predict everything they'll do. Sometimes you'll think they'll be fine and they're not, and sometimes you think they'll be upset and they aren't. They might react how you expect, and they might not. It just means you have to be ready for any outcome. It helps to have a support system in case things go *really* bad, like a place you can go if your parents don't accept you." I paused. "Not that I think that'll happen to you. At least, I hope not."

Talia twisted in my direction, adopting her best puppy-dog eyes. "Will you help me with this?" she asked.

As if she even needed to ask. "Of course," I said. "But first maybe we should take care of the trash for real. Let's talk more after the dance, okay?"

Talia smiled. "It's a date."

The next twenty minutes were a blur as the bunk worked as one, scouring the cabin for any hint of dust or mess. As the clock struck ten, the camp director and his assistant strolled in for inspection. We held our breath as one as they inspected the shelves, rafters, beds and bathroom, awaiting their verdict.

"Take out the trash in the bathroom," said the director. "And I think that you guys are all set. You can head off to the dance." The two men waved goodnight and left us in stunned silence.

Sarah was the first to break it. "YES!" she shouted, pumping her fist. "My bunks never get checked off on the first try! We're going to be on time for the dance! We might even be first!" The rest of the bunk joined in her cheering; the thought of partying for two hours straight was pretty exciting.

After taking care of the bathroom trash as promised, the bunk streamed out the door and to the promised celebration. It was a special night—the ending of the first summer session. Many campers would be going home in the next few days, and tonight was the last night we could all spend time together. I spotted a few of my bunkmates sharing tearful goodbyes with their friends from other bunks, but I didn't pay them too much attention. I was more interested in two things: the sundae buffet being served, and dancing with Talia.

We resumed our conversation at the end of the night, as we made our way toward the cabin. My watch read just a few minutes past midnight, and the moon and stars were our only light.

"So you don't think I should do it?" she asked.

"No," I said. "I don't think you should do it. It's a big deal to come out to your parents, and you need to take some time and consideration for how you want to do it, which, no offense, you haven't."

"None taken. That's why I'm talking about this with you," Talia said.

"I mean, you really don't want to start a big discussion with your parents that you won't be able to finish immediately," I said. "If you tell them tomorrow, they'll definitely have a lot of questions for you. That's just the way parents are. If you're stuck at camp, then you won't be able to talk to them. That gives them an entire month to stew."

Talia pursed her lips. "But what if I think I'm ready to tell them?" she asked. "I want them to know me—the real me, you know? And I want to be able to introduce you as my girlfriend, not just a new friend I met." She looked up at the sky. "What if I just told them right before they left tomorrow? Just like, y'know, right as they're leaving, go, 'Bye Mom, bye Dad, by the way I like girls,' and run back into the bunk before they can say anything."

"You're kidding, right?" I laughed.

"I thought it was funny," Talia pouted.

She was so cute. I elbowed her lightly as we walked. "Seriously, though," I said, "I think you should put more thought into what you want to say when you tell them. I don't think you should rush it, and I really don't want to see you stressing for the next month about what they'll do when they see you again. I get your impatience, but this is something you have to be smart about, you know?"

She sighed. "I know," she said, and I felt a bit guilty. Was I really pressuring her to stay in the closet? Was this the right thing to do? I didn't know. I just knew I didn't want to see her ruin her relationship with her parents because she jumped into this without thinking. Coming out, to family especially, was scary and hard, and I didn't think it was the kind of thing that could be done spur-of-the-moment.

"It's up to you in the end," I reminded her. "If you're going to be a nervous wreck for the rest of the summer because you haven't told them, that's no good. But if you're going to be a nervous wreck because you don't like what they might have to say, that's no good either. If you think you can trust them, then go with your gut and tell them outright. I don't want to force you to stay in the closet. I know that that's a horrible place to be, and that you've definitely had enough of it. There's only one person in the world who could make this decision, and that's you. Go with your heart."

Talia looked at me. "My heart," she said, "is telling me the only way to make you stop talking about this is to kiss you. Maybe I should take its advice?" I laughed as she leaned in to kiss me.

It was sweet, as usual. And then there was a hand on my back, and it wasn't anymore.

We pulled from each other like lightning struck, twisting to see Rachel's disapproving frown. She looked between us, expression unreadable. Finally, she said, "Follow me," and pushed past us into the bunk. Talia and I exchanged fearful looks, took each other's hands, and followed.

Chapter Six

The bunk was dark. Rachel made no move for the light switch, opting instead to guide Talia and me to the back of the bunk in complete darkness. She brought us to her area, and we sat on her bed.

I tried to speak up, but Rachel cut me off. "Whatever you're going to say, I don't want to hear it," she hissed, voice low. Nobody else had returned to the bunk yet, but she kept her voice low anyway. The quiet was worse than if she had been yelling at us. Talia next to me looked to be on the verge of tears.

"Tell me exactly what is going on here," she demanded. "I need to know everything. Everything that's happened, everyone you've told, everything you've done, everything. We need to figure out a way to deal with this, and that starts with honesty." She looked me in the eyes. "Well? Go on. Start."

"Nothing," I said, forcing myself to stay calm. "Nothing happened."

Rachel glared at me. "Don't give me that bullshit," she snarled. "I deserve more than that. I deserve the truth. If I'm going to be able to help you, then I'm going to need the absolute truth."

"We're dating," Talia said. Even in the darkness, I could see the tears beading in the corner of her eyes. I almost put an arm around her, but thought better of it. "No one knows, and no one was supposed to know," she continued. "We don't want to get in trouble. We're good campers, you know that's true. You said you support gay rights. I mean, you said that you don't support the camp's policies. So you're on our side, right? You have to be. No one else is. You saw with your sister what that does to a person. You need to be on our side. Or was everything you said about wanting our happiness just talk?"

Rachel's frown deepened. "I do support gay rights," she said, "and I do think that the camp rules are stupid and outdated. But I am an employee of the camp. My own opinion and the camp's are two separate things. I know that you two are good kids, and I know that you deserve to be here. But the camp isn't going to care. If they find out, you're done here. There's nothing that I, Sarah, your parents, or even the assistant director can do to protect you at that point. You'll get kicked out and be made an example of. You will be used to teach the rest of the campers a lesson, and it doesn't matter if it isn't a good one because it's one they want to teach.

"All of that is going to happen if anyone else finds out you're gay," she continued. "Talia, you're right. I don't agree with the camp's policies, and I want to protect you because that's my responsibility as your counselor. So this is what is going to happen."

I held my breath.

"I'm not going to tell the camp," Rachel said. I exhaled in relief, but then she continued: "And you aren't going to tell anyone else. Not any of the other campers, not any of the other counselors, not any of the staff. No one. If you tell a single person, you're going to get sent home. I can guarantee it."

"Wh—" Talia spluttered. "But—I was going to talk to my parents about—"

"No," Rachel said firmly. "I understand I'm asking a lot of you. I know the closet's an awful place to be. I saw my sister go through the same thing. But this is the only way I can protect you, so please understand." She paused. "Watch yourself too, okay? Hold hands and hug, sure, but not more than everyone else. Sign up for different activities, maybe hang out with other people."

I stared at her in disbelief. We had been doing just fine all summer without her poking her nose into things. I didn't understand why we had to change our behavior all of a sudden. She wouldn't have even noticed if she hadn't caught us kissing. Why did we have to listen to her when we'd been doing just fine on our own? She wasn't helping us. She was just making me angry.

Rachel looked at us both. "I'm sorry I have to do this to you two," she said, voice quiet. "But I promise if you listen to me you'll be able to stay at camp. So just trust me, okay?"

I couldn't see any way that this could turn out for the better if we didn't agree to her conditions. We were lucky that she was as accepting as she was; nearly any other counselor would have simply turned us in without giving it a second thought, sealing our fates.

"Fine," I finally said. "We'll just pretend none of this happened. Is that okay with you, Talia?" She nodded, not meeting my eyes. "Fine. We're both on board."

"Good," Rachel said. "I won't say anything if you guys promise to be more discreet." Again, we nodded. She looked down at her phone. "The rest of the girls are at the waterfront," she told us, like nothing had just happened. "Go join them. Tell Sarah that I'll be there in a minute." And with that we got up and left the bunk, closing the door quietly and tiptoeing our way down to the beach. Talia reached for my hand, but I slapped hers away. For a moment there was silence, and then I heard her release the most dreadful wail I'd ever heard.

I couldn't focus during the activity on the beach. It was something to do with the memories we'd made during the summer, but I wasn't paying attention. Talia and I sat on opposite ends of the beach. When the other girls got up, I did too. When the other girls went back to the bunk, I did too. When the other girls asked me what was wrong, I said nothing. I stood there petrified, my lips closed, damming the avalanche of words that would have cascaded out given half the chance. I locked my gaze on a bunk in the distance to keep from seeing their curious little eyes. I didn't realize I was crying until Sarah came up to me.

"Hey, hey," she said, placing one of her hands reassuringly on my shoulder. "I know that I don't know what's going on right now, but I can tell you that whatever it is will work itself out. Whatever it is can be handled. Things will get better, I promise. Camp is the perfect place to heal from whatever is hurting you, okay?"

"No," I told her. "You're wrong. Camp is what's wrong with me. Camp will not fix it, camp is gonna keep breaking me."

She wrapped me in a hug but didn't say anything more.

That night, for the first time since we began dating, Talia and I didn't snuggle before bed. Instead, we lay in our bunks and cried noiselessly as the other girls went to sleep. I was too numb to tell what I was feeling anymore. Maybe I was just afraid, or maybe there was more to it.

We awoke the next morning at eight o'clock, just as always. Nothing was different, except that everything was different. Everything was changing. We hurriedly got ready, showering, dressing, and scurrying out of the bunk and into the dining hall. We were to say our goodbyes to our first session friends, then return to our bunk for one final cleaning and inspection before our parents arrived. Then we were going to greet our parents with bright smiling faces and tell them that we loved camp more than ever, and never wanted to leave.

Except I did want to leave. More than anything in the world. I wanted to leave more than I did the first moment when I got to camp. The only reason I wasn't going to break down in tears and beg my parents to take me away was Talia. I didn't want to leave her alone for an entire month, trapped in this place that rejected the core of her. My heart ached thinking that I wouldn't get to see her after camp. I wouldn't get to hold her hand or kiss her in the mornings. I wouldn't get to tell her how much she meant to me. I wanted to scream and throw up and cry all at once. I hated being in the camp, but I couldn't leave. I wouldn't leave her behind.

I didn't really have anyone to say goodbye to; most of the girls I hung out with were in my bunk or the other full summer bunk. After breakfast ended, we all went back to our bunks. I began rearranging my shelves for what seemed like at least the millionth time that morning, trying to get everything to fit properly and still look neat and folded. I just knew that my mom would throw a huge fuss if my area didn't look perfect.

Someone touched my shoulder and I jumped. "It's only me," Rachel said, and then, "You don't have to look so annoyed."

I was pretty sure I had every right to be annoyed. Overnight, Rachel had turned herself into the face of everything unfair in my life. She was authority and caregiver and friend all at once, and I knew that she was only doing what she thought was right, and I hated her for it.

Apparently I was easier to read than I thought, because Rachel said, "You can hate me if you want. I understand. I know I'm hurting you right now. But you still need to respect me. I'm doing this for you, you know? I'm trying to protect you and Talia because I don't want to see you thrown out of camp. I don't want to see anything like that happen to my campers." She frowned. "It's bad enough I had to see it happen to my sister."

I said, "I don't need your permission to hate you."

Rachel ignored that. "I needed to ask you something. I'd ask

Talia too, but you seem a little more clearheaded right now. I didn't get a good answer last night and I need to know what's going on. Do I need to reassign one of you to a different bunk, or will you be able to stay in the same bunk and just not be as... as touchy-feely as you might want to be?"

I rolled my eyes. "Are you kidding me?" I scoffed. "Are you like, actually kidding me right now? We haven't been any more touchy than any other girl in this bunk this whole summer. And suddenly you're singling us out because, what? Because we're gay? Because our physical contact means something a little different? You're so hypocritical. You're trying to control us, yet half of these girls sleep in each other's beds and you don't give a damn. That's because you think that they're straight. You assume that they're straight because this camp wants everyone to be."

I twisted away to keep Rachel from seeing the tears welling up in my eyes. I was just so frustrated with it all. I threw myself on my bed, not caring what the other girls saw or what they thought. None of it mattered. Not in that moment.

Rachel sat down on the bed next to me and rubbed my back. I was too exhausted to pull away, so I just let her do it. After a moment she moved on to stroking my hair. It reminded me of my own mother so much that my tears sprang anew. In that moment, I was little more than a child, incapable of dealing with my problems maturely. Then again, the camp wasn't dealing with their problems in a very mature way, either.

After a minute, Rachel murmured, "You should get up and rinse your face." I didn't move. "The parents are gonna be here any minute now. I want you to look happy, even if you're not. I don't want you to leave, and I don't want you to feel like you have to. I especially don't want your parents to feel like you need to leave. Are you going to be okay?"

I wanted to scream, *Of course I'm not going to be okay!* I wasn't okay, and I didn't feel like I would ever be okay again. All Rachel cared about was the stupid camp; how the camp would react, how the camp would look if parents pulled a full-summer camper halfway through the session. I wanted to yell and flail and shout like a child throwing a tantrum.

But I remembered Talia. And I remembered that I didn't want to leave her alone.

So I wiped my face, said, "I'll be fine," and returned to rearranging my shelves.

Chapter Seven

My parents arrived around eleven thirty. They weren't the last ones there, but I had been waiting for almost an hour after the rest of my bunkmates' parents got there. Rather than wait outside with the rest of the bunk, I chose to wait inside to give myself a little more time to mope.

I pretended to sleep as I heard footsteps, and then I felt a hand at my back and my mother's voice saying, "Reina, sweetie, wake up."

I wiped my face on the pillow before I raised my head in greeting. I had to be strong. I didn't fully understand why in that moment, but I knew that I had to be strong.

"Hi Mom, hi Dad," I said. As they hugged me, I felt more tears come forth. I couldn't help it; it had been so long since I'd seen them, and the night before had been the most stressful experience of my life.

"Oh, sweetheart," my mom said, "it's okay. We missed you too. I know that it must have been hard for you, being away from home for the first time like this. We are both so proud of you for sticking it out. Are you having fun?" she asked hopefully. I nodded, in spite of myself.

My dad tousled my hair gently. "We missed you, kiddo. We really did." I knew it must have been hard for them too; it was my first time away from home, and their first time away from me. I owed it to them to at least pretend like I was alright.

I sat upright on my bed. "You guys must be tired and hungry from the trip, why don't we go into town and grab something to eat? I hear there's a pretty good pizza place in town."

"Why don't we take a brief tour of the camp first?" my

dad suggested. "I haven't been here in years; I wonder what's changed. I can show you my old bunks!" He looked very excited at the idea. "And you can introduce me to all of you friends and counselors. The pictures that you're in on the website are all with another girl, the one with dark curly hair. Are you guys close, or just photogenic?"

I pretended to laugh at his joke. "Yeah, um, I guess that you could say that she and I are pretty close. I mean, I wouldn't call us best friends, or anything." Even though I was out to my parents, I couldn't tell them I was dating Talia. Not with Rachel breathing down my neck. I was too afraid. Plus, I didn't really know what my future with Talia looked like. I didn't want to tell them just yet anyway.

"So," I continued. "Pizza?"

After convincing my parents that the only way to beat the crowds was to go into town now and tour the camp later, they led me to the car. Truth be told, I didn't feel like dealing with my parents right then, but then again, I didn't feel like dealing with anyone. In the safety of the family car, I let myself fall apart a bit. I told them about what I could. They asked me what I was doing, my friends, the counselors, and about just about any other question they could think of. They told me repeatedly that they missed me, and I used that as my excuse to cry. That I just really missed them, and it was good to see them again. For the most part, I think that they bought it.

"So," my father started after a moment of silence. "Are there any special young ladies we should know about? This camp is really into matchmaking, after all. They've always been very supportive of your mother and me and our relationship. They were so excited when I told them that you were coming."

I laughed despite myself. "Are you kidding me?" I said. "This camp is awful when it comes to gay issues. They even have a policy that says that any staff members or campers that come out get fired or sent home or whatever. No one even knows that I'm gay."

My dad gave me a puzzled look. "Well, that *was* the policy, true," he said, "but they changed it."

I blinked. "What?"

"The new assistant director made a huge stink about it, so the camp reversed their policies. They just never made any big public announcement about their decision because their old policies were never explicitly stated. Are people giving you trouble about being gay?" Now he looked concerned.

I stared at him. "What are you talking about?" I said. "As far as I know the policies are still in place. I haven't told anyone I'm gay because I'd get kicked out. I was just talking with my counselor about this the other day, and she said the policies hadn't changed."

"Yes they have," he said. "I was literally just talking about this with another camp alum. We were talking about how his kid is also gay, and is out at the Camp Geshem in Pennsylvania. Is that why you're so upset, Reina? Because you haven't been able to be yourself?" My silence confirmed my parents' suspicions.

"Oh honey," my mom said. It wasn't condescending, but full of pity. Rage burned in my gut, and all of it was directed at Rachel. For whatever reason, she had lied to us. She had hurt me and Talia so much, and for what? Nothing?

I hardly spoke during lunch as we chewed through pizza that was way more mediocre than I'd thought it would be. My parents asked more questions, and I only volunteered the bare minimum of information to satisfy their curiosity. They filled me in on some news that had happened at home, but I wasn't paying attention. I couldn't.

First, I was angry. I'd been forced to lie about myself all summer. I had to hide who I was all summer. My own counselor had lied to me. Then I was hopeful. Maybe I could be honest with everyone. Maybe I could tell them about me, and maybe Talia could come out too, and everything could be in the open and we wouldn't have to hide anymore.

I made my decision: I was going to tell the bunk that very night. I wouldn't let myself get intimidated, and I wouldn't permit myself to be afraid. I would tell them who I was, and whether they accepted me or not was up to them. It didn't matter to me. I just wanted to be me—the whole of me, not a sanitized version of myself I pretended to be.

The feeling following my decision was liberating. I started to plan out what I would say to them, word by precious word. I was excited that the girls of Chaverim Bunk Four would get to know the real me. Just the night before, I had been so distraught. This gave me hope. This gave me the reason I needed to stay at camp.

I got away with giving my parents little more than a brief tour of the camp, getting them out before they had the chance to meet with my counselors or bunkmates. I had other things on my mind, like how I would come out and when. I wanted to do it after dinner, just before our evening bunk activity.

Dinner came sooner than I thought. I sat with Talia, ignoring Rachel's annoyed stare from across the room, and asked her about her parents.

"It was nice seeing them again," she said absently. "I mean, I'm still upset, but it was nice to hang out with them and forget about all that for the afternoon." She frowned. "I'm still pissed at Rachel." I nodded in agreement. "I mean, I know she's right and that we have to be careful. But we've *been* careful. She just happened to be sneaking around last night at an inopportune time. It wasn't our fault, and she shouldn't be restricting us. Did you see the way that she glared at you when you came over to sit next to me? I mean, what's up with that?"

"It's stupid," I agreed, "but that's not what I want to talk to you about. I leaned in and lowered my voice to a murmur. "I was talking to my dad today. The whole policy about gay campers was reversed at the start of the summer."

Talia's eyes widened. "You're kidding."

"It's true," I said. "The decision hasn't been made public though. You know what this means, right? We can come out if we want to. We can be out as a couple. We don't have to hide anything."

I wasn't sure how Talia would take this news, but her face broke out into a huge smile. "That's amazing," she whispered. "Best news in the world."

"So do you want to tell the bunk?"

"Of course I do!" Talia's eyes sparkled. "I mean, if we can't get in trouble for it, why not, you know? When do you want to tell people?"

I smiled back at her. "I was thinking of doing it tonight during the bunk activity. Is that alright with you?"

"Sounds good." Talia looked pleased. "Plus we already have an idea of how everyone will react, right? When we talked about the policy change earlier this summer everyone was in favor of it. Nobody reacted badly to the idea. I think they'll all be supportive of us."

"What about your parents? Do you still want to tell them?"

Talia's smile vanished, and that was enough of an answer for me, but I waited for her to speak anyway. "Not yet," she said. "I… I don't think I'm ready just yet."

I nodded. "Whatever works for you."

We held hands as we walked to the bunk after dinner. I didn't have to look to feel Rachel's gaze boring holes into my back, but I didn't care. For once, we could be openly happy. It seemed that everything around us was happy too. The sunset filled the sky with reds and pinks and yellows, the crickets offered their voices to the natural symphony of the woods, and we were going to be okay.

We'd discussed the plan briefly over dinner; I'd had more time to think about it, since I'd heard the news at lunch. We knew the bunk activity that evening was going to be a simple recap of what we'd done during Parent Day. At the end of it, we were going to make the announcement and that would be that. Maybe it wasn't the most sophisticated plan, but considering the short notice it was a pretty good one.

We were the last to join in on the circle, and once we were seated, Rachel began. "I hope you all had a good Parent Day," she said. "I know I did. I got to see my dog and ate some amazing ice cream." Laughter rippled around the circle. "Let's go around the circle and talk about what we did today. Who we spent time with, what we did, what we liked, and any news from home. Sarah, why don't you start?"

The discussion went around the circle, with each person rattling off a brief list of their experiences of the day. The discussion slowly got closer to me and Talia, and I could feel her tensing in anticipation. I didn't blame her. I was nervous too. Nervous, but excited. Freedom was just a few short minutes away.

Finally, Rachel was saying, "Talia, your turn." Talia took my hand, and I squeezed it back. She looked around the circle, took a deep breath, and began to speak.

"I don't want to talk about my Parent Day," she said. Rachel's eyes narrowed, but Talia continued. "I mean, it was fine, but that's not what I want to talk about with you guys. You've all known me for a while, and over the last few years I've really grown to see you as my family. I've been lucky enough to get close to all of you in particular this year, and I'm really happy about that. It makes me want to be completely honest with you all, so I need to tell you something important about myself."

"Talia," Rachel said, voice low in warning, but she didn't stop.

"I like girls," Talia declared. "I like them in the same way I like guys. I don't want to hide that part of myself from you anymore, and… well, I think it's important you all know because Reina and I started dating this year."

You could hear a pin drop in the cabin. Every eye was turned on us, every mouth was hung open in shock. Sarah didn't seem to know what to make of us.

Rachel hissed, "What are you doing?" I ignored her. Even if she didn't know about the new rules, they were still in place. She couldn't do anything.

"I also like girls," I said. "If that wasn't, y'know, obvious. I'm out at home, but I didn't want to tell you guys because of the policy and everything. You've all made me feel comfortable since the first day at camp, and I appreciate it a lot, which is why I decided to tell you."

A few of the girls began to bubble over with questions, but Rachel cut them off. "What the hell are you two doing?" she demanded. "I told you, you couldn't tell anyone. You're going to get sent home, and you're going to get me fired! I thought you'd be smarter about this, what the hell are you doing!?"

"Rachel?" Sarah said tentatively, but Rachel ignored her, pacing about the cabin.

"I mean, seriously? It hasn't even been a full day since I talked to you. Are you trying to get sent home? This is going to completely derail any conversation about a rule change. You're just adding heat to a dying fire. What are you thinking?"

I stood my ground. "I was talking to my dad earlier today. He said that Camp Geshem changed its policy at the beginning of the summer but it wasn't made public. So it's fine, right? It has to be."

Rachel looked frustrated to the point of tears. "No, Reina," she said furiously, "it's *not* fine. *Some* Camp Geshems have changed their policy. There's one in Connecticut that did. But not this one."

The truth hit me like a sack of bricks. I felt hollow. "What...?"

"All that's changed," Rachel went on, "is that I can't protect you anymore. You really will be sent home this time, and there's nothing I can do about it."

The rest of the cabin looked between us, unsure of what to do or say. I glanced at Talia beside me; the color had drained from her face completely, and her horrified expression probably mirrored my own. We were going to be sent home. We were going to be sent home, and never come back.

I'd been trying to earn us our freedom. Instead, I'd doomed us both.

Chapter Eight

There was a nasty taste in my mouth the next morning.

I hadn't thrown up, but I wished I had. My whole face felt puffy from crying. I didn't remember much else from the night before, aside from the girls in the bunk trying to offer me and Talia some comfort. I felt awful. I'd pressured her into coming out when she wasn't ready, and her first experience with it had been a disaster thanks to me. And now we were both going to be sent home, and it was all my fault.

I looked at my watch; it was insanely early. I didn't need to be up for at least another two hours. I didn't feel like I could fall back asleep, so I climbed out of my bed and into Talia's. No one noticed, but even if they had, who cared? We'd already told them, and we were already in trouble. What was the worst that could happen?

I wasn't surprised to see Talia awake too. She looked at me blearily before lifting the covers as an invitation. I climbed in, and she gave me a peck on the cheek before turning over and falling back asleep. I wished I could have done the same. Instead, I lay there, a thousand thoughts racing through my mind and yet I was unable to think of anything at all. There was so much uncertainty right now. The only thing I was certain about was that I was going home.

I took in the beauty that was Talia, and then I let everything else go. I focused only on her, on her each breath, and the rise and fall her chest. I focused on her each individual curl, and the fact that even in a cold bunk early in the morning, her cheeks were pink with a flush. I reached under the covers for her hand, and then laced my fingers between hers.

Finally, sleep came, but it was short. I awoke to Sarah shaking my shoulder. "Reina," she said softly, "you need to get back to your own bed. I know it's early and it's cold, but if the girls see you sleeping in the same bed and any of them are interviewed by the administration it's not going to be good."

"It's already not going to be good," I said. "It's all screwed up."

Sarah pursed her lips. "I know," she replied. "I know it's hard to believe right now, but you need to believe that it'll all work out. The people who run this camp know what they're doing, and everyone in this bunk really loves you. We're going to do everything in our power to keep you here, but you need to go back to your own bed."

I groaned, but did as I was told. I knew that this day was going to be hell, but it didn't have to start with me fighting one of the few people who was left on my side. As I lay in my bed, waiting through the last few moments before the official wake-up call, I reflected on what today would bring. Talia and I were going to go with Sarah and Rachel to the camp office to speak to the director and assistant director. We were going to come clean to them about our relationship and tell them we wanted to stay at the camp regardless of the rules. I'd thought of a few talking points already, but I didn't want to think about them now. All I wanted to do in that moment was climb back into bed with Talia, soak in her warmth.

I heard Rachel's alarm go off. She swung from her bed a few minutes later and lumbered to the bathroom while Sarah, already showered and dressed, prepared for the day. After a brief shower, Rachel returned and began playing music from her phone loud enough for the whole bunk to hear. It only took two or three songs before the entire cabin was abuzz with movement, with girls rolling from their beds and pulling on clothes and falling into morning routines. Looking at the scene, you wouldn't think something so dramatic had happened the night before.

I climbed out of bed. The longer I waited, the worse I was going to feel. I moved about the cabin with my blanket wrapped around my shoulders, getting dressed and ready for the day. Eventually, I spied movement from Talia's bed. She sat up, looking groggy and not fully awake. After a minute or two she climbed down and our eyes met.

"Well," she said, "been nice knowing you. Since, you know, we're gonna die today."

"Not funny," I said, even though I was smiling.

"To each their own. I personally think I'm hilarious." Talia yawned. "I do some of my best work when I'm scared stiff."

"We're going to be okay," I said, even though I didn't believe it.

"Mm." Talia scrunched her eyes. "Guess we gotta keep saying that, huh."

We both dressed modestly for the day; we were doing our best not to get kicked out of camp, and we didn't want to give them a reason to mark us up for not following dress code. I could feel the eyes of the other girls in the bunk on us as we prepared for the day, but I tried not to think about it. I was already nervous enough.

Breakfast was hard. My stomach was doing too many flips for me to feel that I could keep anything down. I settled for a few bites of toast and some mouthfuls of water. Talia wasn't doing much better than I was; I watched her push her eggs around with a fork and only manage half a glass of orange juice. Neither of us knew what to expect, and we didn't know how well it would go, if it would go well at all.

Sarah, Rachel, Talia, and I stayed behind outside the mess hall as breakfast finished. We watched the other girls return to the cabin, where they would be cleaning some more while

Talia and I pled our case and tried not to face the humiliation of being sent home for breaking the rules in such a stupid way. A few of the girls wished us luck before leaving.

After saying our goodbyes, we began to head toward the office. I fell in line with Talia and took her hand. "What do you think is going to happen?" I asked. I knew that the outcome was more than likely going to be a grim one, but everything she had said so far had been positive. I wanted to know whether or not she truly believed it, or if she was just trying to comfort me and herself.

She gave me a mournful look. "It's not going to be good. I am an optimist, through and through, you know that. I pride myself on it. I always think that situations are going to produce the best possible outcomes, but I know that we don't have much of a chance for a positive outcome. It's simply not an option. We need to prepare ourselves. No matter what happens, we'll know soon enough."

On that cheery note, we arrived at the camp office, climbing the steps and entering the lobby. Rachel spoke to the secretary to let her know we'd arrived for our appointment with the director and assistant director, and then there was nothing to do but wait. I fidgeted in the silence, running through all the talking points I'd come up with. I was sure I'd thought of everything, but would it be enough? What if I had missed something? What if they didn't let me speak in the first place? Would they even be willing to listen to me?

My anxious thoughts were put on hold as the secretary called for us. We followed her through the hall to the director's office, with Rachel leading the pack, the rest of us following behind like ducklings.

"Good morning, Director," Rachel said to the man behind the desk. I recognized him and the man next to him; they'd visited Saturday night for the bunk inspection. The four of us took turns shaking hands before we lapsed into awkward silence.

"Please, please," said the director, "just call me Ezra. I'm not the president or anything. What can I do for you lovely ladies on this fine morning?"

The four of us exchanged uncomfortable glances. Sarah was the first to speak.

"As counselors," she began, "we have certain responsibilities. At this camp in particular, one of those major responsibilities that Rachel and I take very seriously is reporting to the camp's administration when rules are broken, especially when those who have broken them come clean to us. These two girls formed…" She trailed off for a minute, looking at us and then back to the men. "They started a relationship earlier in the summer, and they told us about it last night. We wanted to address it head-on with your help, so we decided that it would be best to bring them here for a meeting with the two of you. To talk about options that both they and the camp have with how to deal with this."

The director and the assistant director nodded, soaking in the information but saying nothing. I couldn't read their faces. When it became clear that Sarah had nothing else to say, the assistant director began to speak. He said, "I probably don't have to tell you this, but this camp does not have a great history when it comes to LGBTQ campers and staff members. One of my primary goals when I came to work here was to change that. Luckily for your campers, I have. Starting with the next session later in the week, our camp's policy regarding LGBTQ campers and staff is over. We completely abolished it. Normally we wait to enact new policies at the beginning of the summer, but we were still discussing different options we had for this at the beginning of the summer and throughout first session.

The board finally made their decision last week and we decided that we didn't want to wait until next summer. We didn't want to punish any more campers for feeling comfortable here and being open about who they are. What that means for you guys," he said, shifting his gaze to look at me and Talia, "is that you're off the hook for this. We're not going to send you home, we aren't going to call your parents, and we are definitely not going to embarrass you. This camp totally has your back on this and I hope that you two girls are happy together."

Talia and I stared at him, dumbfounded. This was the opposite outcome we'd expected. It wasn't even something we'd thought would be a possibility. We could just… stay? No strings attached? Nothing was going to happen because of what we'd done? Because of what *I* had done? I didn't realize how fast my heart had been beating until it slowed down, didn't realize how tense I'd been until I relaxed. Maybe everything was going to be okay.

And then Ezra said, "Unfortunately…" and my heart sank.

"Because the two of you are in a relationship, and because you're in the same bunk, one of you will need to change bunks. I know that this isn't ideal, especially partway through the summer, but that is part of the new policy. We can't be monitoring you all the time, and after all, we wouldn't let a boy sleep in a girls' bunk."

I flushed with indignation. "It's not the same thing," I spluttered. "You wouldn't let a boy sleep in the girls' bunk because he's a different gender." Rachel shot me a look but I didn't care. I kept going. "We don't need to be monitored all the time. We're mature enough to understand what's appropriate and what's not. If you ask me, this is just a way to punish us. There's no reason to separate us. You're just making this up."

Sarah stared at me in shock. For their part, Ezra and the

assistant director didn't look surprised or upset; they seemed to take my outburst just fine.

"Bill?" Ezra said, glancing at the assistant director. "You got this?" Bill nodded, and the director stood up and left. He turned to look at me. I almost regretted saying what I had, but at the same time, I didn't want my concerns to go unvoiced. I was not one to suffer in silence.

"I'm glad that you feel passionately about this," Bill said. "I'm passionate about it too, which is why I've been pushing for this change since I was hired. Luckily, it happened. That's why you get to stay here. Unfortunately, one of the conditions of the rules being abolished was that campers in a relationship could not be in the same bunk. I know that this seems unfair, but it's much fairer than making you go home, outing you to everyone at camp, your parents, and your entire community, and humiliating you in the process. We changed the outdated policy for people like you, who love camp and don't want to sacrifice their happiness and well-being while they're here. Maybe in a few years, there'll be change again. For now, this is the best I can do. Try to focus on the positives, and be happy that you can stay at camp."

With that, he stood and showed us the door. Tears burned in my eyes, but I refused to let any of them spill out and onto my face until after we had left the building.

Once we were a safe distance away from it all, the tears poured out of me. I desperately tried to force air into my body, but no matter how much I swallowed it didn't fill up my lungs. I heard shouting. I think Talia grabbed me in some attempt at comfort, but it didn't help. The world spun, and the ground came up to meet me, and everything went dark.

Chapter Nine

I woke up in the camp infirmary.

I stared at the ceiling, trying to piece together what had happened. I vaguely recalled panicked expressions, hysterical shouts, being carried. I think someone screamed for help. Now I was lying on a scratchy cot in a small white room, with the air conditioner blasting. A woman worked at a desk nearby; I recognized her as the camp nurse.

She noticed my movement and turned toward me. "Welcome back to the land of the living," she said. "Seems you had a pretty nasty panic attack if it made you pass out like that. Are you feeling any better?"

I nodded. "A little." I began to sit up, but she put a hand on my shoulder.

"You should stay lying down for the time being," she said gently. "You need to rest for now." She checked her clipboard. "The girls who brought you here are in the waiting room. Would you like me to go get them?"

"Yes, please."

She nodded and left. A moment later Talia appeared in the doorway, followed by Rachel and Sarah. Talia rushed over, worry plain in her expression.

"Are you okay?" she whispered. "I—I didn't know what to do, you just started shaking and you weren't responding to anything I said, a-and then you went all limp and still and I just—I started freaking out, I thought—"

"I'm fine," I assured her. "I'm really fine. I just need to rest for a while." I paused. "I haven't had a panic attack that bad in… a long time, but if I take it easy for the rest of the day I'll be alright."

"Are you sure?"

"Yes." She was such a worrywart. It was cute.

"Can I…" Talia played with her fingers. "Can I hug you then?"

I opened my arms in response. She squeezed me tightly, and it was comforting to be squished in such a way.

"I was so scared," Talia sniffled. Then she began to cry, and I started to cry too. I'd cried too many times in the last few days to be embarrassed about it anymore, but Rachel and Sarah were still right here, so I tried to hide as much of it as I could. Thankfully, they looked in the other direction and waited for us to finish.

When we were done, Sarah said, "The nurse talked to us. She said as long as you drink plenty of fluids and get some rest, you'll be alright. Talia had her arms around you when you fell and she kind of cushioned your fall. We'll make sure you get some food at the bunk, so don't worry about having to go to the mess hall or anything."

"Thanks," I said. "I appreciate it."

She shrugged. "We look after our campers, remember?"

"Heh, yeah." Now that I could think again, the memory of the conversation at the office returned. One of us would be leaving Chaverim Four soon, and that reality was a bitter pill to swallow.

Talia led me out of the infirmary and into the sunshine. We returned to the bunk and I spent most of the day lying down and resting, with Talia visiting me frequently and Sarah or Rachel bringing me food from the mess hall. For most of the day I was left alone with my thoughts, reflecting on the events as of late. Now that I'd calmed down, I could see that while it was frustrating, being in a different bunk than Talia wasn't going to be the end of the world. All that was going to change was where one of us slept. We would still be in the camp, and we could still do activities together. It just wouldn't be as many activities as I'd like it to be. We would still see each other at meals, and we could coordinate our electives, and we could spend our free time with each other. I would miss her, but it wouldn't be all bad.

Rachel took me to the infirmary shortly after dinner, mentioning that the nurse wanted to do a checkup. I insisted I could go back to the bunk by myself, and she conceded after the nurse assured her I would be fine.

I sat on the cot I had woken up on earlier as the nurse checked my temperature and pulse. "Have you been dizzy since this morning?" she asked. I shook my head. "Good, that's good. Nausea? Headaches? Lightheadedness?" I shook my head to all her questions. "Wonderful. And you've been drinking plenty of water all day?" I nodded. "Great. Good girl."

The nurse paused, looking at her clipboard. She frowned. "Oh, shoot," she said.

"Is there something wrong?" I asked.

"No, just an oversight on my part," the nurse said. "Looks like no one called your parents to mention your fainting spell. The camp should've done that earlier... I don't know how that slipped between the cracks." She looked up at me. "Would you like to call your parents now?"

I bit my lip, weighing the pros and cons. On the one hand, I wasn't sure if I wanted to talk to them right now. On the other, I would rather they hear about what happened from me instead of one of the camp faculty. And more than that, I wanted to tell them what happened. The whole truth of it, not the watered-down version.

"Sure," I said.

The nurse nodded and led me to her office, where she showed me her office phone and explained how to dial outside the camp. Fortunately I had my home phone number memorized, and though I was worried I'd entered the wrong number at first, my mother picked up on the third ring.

"Hello?" she said.

"Hi, Mom," I replied. I didn't think I would have felt so relieved to hear her voice; I'd seen her in person just the day before.

"Reina? Is that you? What's wrong, sweetheart?"

I laughed a little. "I'm okay, Mom, really. I mean, I'm calling from the infirmary, so I guess I'm not all okay, but I'm okay, I promise."

"The infirmary?" She sounded alarmed. "What happened?"

"Where do I begin," I sighed. "Well, for starters, there's this girl named Talia..."

I began talking about everything that had happened. How I'd started seeing Talia partway through the session, how Rachel had caught us, how we decided to come out, the confusion around the rule change and the subsequent verdict from the assistant director, and my resulting panic attack and fainting spell. It was a relief to get it all off my chest to someone I knew would understand.

When I finished, the other end was quiet. I thought maybe I'd hung up by accident until I heard her exhale. "I'm so sorry," she said. "We really did think the rules had changed. I'm glad you haven't been expelled from camp, but I'm sorry you had to go through all that trouble because of our misunderstanding."

"It's okay, Mom."

"And you're sure you're feeling alright? You did say you passed out."

"I'm fine, Mom."

"If you need me I can still come and get—"

"I'm *fine*, Mom, really. I just wanted to tell you what happened myself."

"I'm sorry, sweetie. I'm your mother and I worry. It's my job." She laughed a bit. "I'm sorry to hear you have to switch bunks, but I'm very happy to know you don't have to leave the camp. Make sure to call again if anything else happens, alright?"

"I will, Mom," I said.

"And be sure to introduce us to Talia when we come to pick you up."

"Mom."

She laughed. "Have a good night, sweetie."

"You too, Mom. Don't worry too much." I knew this was a vain plea. She was a Jewish mother. Worrying was practically in her DNA.

I hung up the phone and thanked the nurse before heading out of the infirmary. To my surprise, Talia was standing outside, waiting. She looked up as I exited.

"I asked Rachel where you'd gone and she said you were here," she said. "I wanted to walk back with you."

I smiled and offered her my hand. "Sounds fine to me."

She took it and smiled back, and everything was alright.

When we returned to the bunk, Sarah was waiting for both of us outside. "I have good news," she announced, "and I have bad news. Which do you want first?"

I said, "Bad news. Tell me what sucks first and what's okay later."

Sarah laughed a bit. "If you insist," she chuckled. "Bad news first, then. I've been talking with the camp admin and other counselors all day. You guys already know one of you is moving to Chaverim Three for the rest of the summer session." We held our breath. "The new campers are going to be here tomorrow morning, and…" She turned to me. "Reina, you're going to move in with them." She looked apologetic. "I'm sorry you guys didn't get to decide who would be switching bunks, but it came down to logistics. Are you okay so far?"

I was disappointed, but I nodded. Talia, on the other hand, didn't seem satisfied. "Why her?" she demanded. "Why does it have to be Reina that moves? I'll do it. It won't matter if I have to switch bunks. I've been here longer anyway, so I'll probably know some of the girls coming tomorrow."

Sarah shook her head. "You're sweet, Talia, really, but we've already worked it out," she said. "We think Reina should switch because the bunk is going to be mostly new campers, so everyone in there will be having a fresh start, not just her. You could start over without any... problems."

Talia frowned. "That wouldn't give me any problems. I'm friends with all the other kids in Chaverim. I wouldn't have to start all over like Reina would."

"I don't think she means that kind of problem," I interrupted. "I'm pretty sure she's talking about homophobia."

Talia blanched. "Oh."

Sarah nodded. "Talia, the girls in Four haven't said anything because we asked them not to. We wanted to give you both the option to go back in the closet if it makes you more comfortable, because we don't want you to get harassed. We know that the girls in Four are fine with who you are, but we also know that not everyone is so accepting. That's all we wanted to do—we just wanted to give you options."

I said, "I appreciate it, but I wouldn't have risked being sent home by coming out if I wanted to go back into the closet after. It's awful in there. It feels like I'm lying to everyone, and most important it feels like I'm lying to myself." I turned to Talia. "Talia, I don't know what you want to do. You can decide for yourself. But I don't want that. I know how to deal with the shit some idiots give you, and I'd rather do that than lie to everyone for another session."

"I don't want that either," Talia said. I was surprised at the quickness of her answer. I'd thought she might have considered Sarah's offer, but it didn't seem like it. "I don't want to lie either, and besides, this isn't something we can take back. Even if the girls in Four have been told not to tell anyone, they still might. They could have already. And even if they don't mean to, they might say something that gets the rumor mill turning. It won't lead to anything good in the end. So I don't want to do that either."

Sarah nodded. "I'll let Rachel know. But Reina, you'll still be switching bunks. I know it'll be a little rough for a few days while you adjust, and that it'll be lonely at first, but I know you're strong enough to get through it." She paused. "We were so afraid you two were going to be sent home. I'm glad it turned out okay."

I checked my watch; it was much later than I'd expected. "It's our last night together," I said. "Can we just… you know, hang out as a bunk? So I can say goodbye?"

Sarah smiled. "That's exactly what I had planned," she said. She invited us in, called the rest of the girls into a circle, and we spent the night chatting and laughing just as we'd done almost every night of camp, as if nothing had changed at all.

Chapter Ten

"Welcome to Camp Geshem!"

Leah, my new counselor, was a petite girl with a voice that seemed a little too big for her small body. Her exclamation drew the attention of the whole bunk. "Please come and sit in the center of the bunk. We're going to do some icebreakers!"

Several of the girls groaned in response, but they sat down anyway. I joined them, comforted by the fact that they were just as new to the group as I was. It almost felt like my first day at camp all over again. In a lot of ways, it was.

"So, how much does a polar bear weigh?" Leah asked. She was met with an awkward silence, which she eventually filled with, "Enough to break the ice!"

The silence that followed was even more awkward, until I broke it with laughter. I couldn't help it; the last few days had been a rollercoaster of tension and nerves. I was relieved to laugh some of it off with a terrible joke. Somehow, my laughter was contagious, and the rest of the girls followed suit, easing the atmosphere of the bunk into something far more pleasant. For her part, Leah looked pleased.

"With that out of the way," she said, "Let's go around the circle and say our names, how long we've been coming to camp, and a fun fact about ourselves. I'll start. My name is Leah, I've been coming here for eight years, and I can speak four languages: English, Spanish, Italian, and Hebrew."

I spoke up from across the circle. "¿Hablas Español?" She looked up at me in surprise. "¿De verdad?"

Leah grinned. "¡Claro que sí!" she exclaimed, laughing. "¿Te mentiría?"

"What are you two saying?" one of the girls spoke up. "I don't understand."

Leah laughed a bit. "She asked me if I really did speak Spanish and I asked her why I would lie about it," she translated. "It's very exciting to meet someone that can speak the same language as you, especially when that language isn't English." She gestured to the girl on her left. "Why don't you go next?"

"Sure," the girl said. "My name is Marissa, and this is my fifth year here. Um, I guess I have a show dog? He's a poodle and my family enters him in competitions, but he doesn't behave so we never win."

The girl to her left went next. "My name is Ariella, it's my seventh year, and I also have a poodle."

Then the girl to her left. "My name is Miri, this is my first year, and I've never left the country."

"I'm Gwen, this is my first summer..."

"Shira, this is my second..."

"Rachelle..."

"Lilly..."

"Sivan..."

"Olivia, but you can call me Ollie..."

"Tzipporah, but everyone calls me Zippy..."

Finally, it was my turn. I'd listened to each introduction, thought about what I was going to say. I could say I was adopted, but that was old news. I could say that I was the only one in the room who had already been in the camp for one session. Or I could be honest.

I decided to go with being honest.

"My name is Reina," I said as all eyes turned to me. "It means 'queen' in Spanish. This is my first summer here, but I was here for the first session too. My fun fact is I'm gay." A few heads that had been drifting away snapped to attention. Even Leah, the counselor, looked surprised. I continued, "I was in Chaverim Four last session, but I had to move because I'm seeing a girl who's also in that bunk. The camp changed its policy regarding gay campers, but since it doesn't allow for us to be in the same bunk I had to move. So now I'm here. Hi."

The silence didn't last nearly as long as I feared it would. "Hardcore," Ollie spoke up. "I have two moms and we were all excited when they heard that stupid policy got overturned. Like, there's already so much hate in the world, we shouldn't have to deal with it at camp. Especially a Jewish camp, like, the whole world has been trying to kill us forever, so we shouldn't be turning on each other. It's really stupid."

I smiled at Ollie. "I'm glad there's other people who are so passionate about this sort of thing."

The other counselor said her piece (Tamar-but-call-her-Tammy, ten years at camp, spent a semester in South Africa), and then she said, "That's all for now, so you guys can start unpacking if you don't have any questions."

I raised my hand. "Actually, I was wondering if I could…" I hesitated, but I'd already talked about my idea with the other counselors. Leah and Tammy both nodded. "Like I said earlier, I'm gay. So if anyone has questions to ask me or misconceptions to clear up, you can just kinda… ask now, I guess?"

Several people looked away, and I wondered if this was a good idea. Then, Ollie spoke up.

"How old were you when you figured out you were gay?" she asked.

I was pretty sure she just asked to keep me from feeling awkward, but I was grateful nonetheless. "It's different for everyone," I said, "but for me it was when I was twelve. I realized I just kept getting crushes on girls instead of guys."

There was silence again, until Leah asked a question. "How

out of the closet are you? Are you okay if people outside this bunk know?"

"I'm open with my parents, but not the rest of my family since they're pretty conservative. I'm out at the camp as well." Which was putting it lightly. "I wasn't going to come out at first, but after I met my girlfriend and we started dating, things just sort of… escalated."

"Do you like boys too?" This was Miri. I'd been expecting a question like this.

"No," I said. "Some people like boys, some like girls, some like both and some like neither." I shrugged. "There's a whole spectrum that people can fall under. I only like girls right now, but I think I used to like boys too. People just change."

"What was coming out for the first time like?" Shira asked.

I considered the question. "I came out to my best friend at school. I asked her to meet me in the library and told her that I was bi—back then I was still trying to convince myself I was into guys. I was really nervous the whole time, my hands were shaking and everything. I could barely get my voice out… so she didn't even hear what I said. I panicked and said it louder, except it came out way louder than I thought it would and the whole library heard me." The circled laughed. "Nobody cared too much. We were all too busy studying for midterms."

"I have a question," Zippy announced. "Are you attracted to us?"

This was the question I'd been dreading the most, but it was also one I needed to answer if I was going to be myself and be comfortable sharing a living space with all these unfamiliar people. Zippy didn't look too keen on sleeping in the same room as someone like me. Besides, even if she hadn't asked the question, it was one that would have been on everyone's minds. All I could do was answer as politely as possible.

"I'm glad you asked," I said, doing my best to keep my voice polite. "I'm not attracted to every girl, just like I'm sure you aren't attracted to every boy."

I thought that would be enough, but Zippy pursued me. "You're dating a girl that used to be in your bunk, right?" I stared at her blankly, and she went on. "You and her started as bunkmates, but you were attracted to her and now you're dating. So, like, how do we know that you won't be attracted to us and look at us when we're changing and stuff?"

As frustrating as it was, I maintained my composure. Leah frowned and opened her mouth, but she closed it as I began to speak. "We started as friends," I explained, patient. "We hung out a lot, and got close. First I was emotionally attracted, and then physically after I knew she was interested. I don't allow myself to see my bunkmates as potential girlfriends because I don't want to make anyone uncomfortable. I take care to turn away when others are changing, because I want people to be comfortable. But in the same way I want you all to be comfortable, I want to be comfortable too."

Zippy frowned, but I kept going. "I want to be respected and not gossiped about. I don't want to be talked about behind my back. That's why I want you to ask me questions. I want you to understand me. I want to understand you. I've been afraid a lot this summer, and I don't want anyone else to feel the same way. I think if we're all open with each other, and if we're kind, we can become good friends, and maybe when we leave, the world will be a little less scary."

I looked around the bunk, warmed by the approving looks I received. Even Zippy looked grudgingly impressed. "Well-spoken, Reina," Leah said. "With that, girls, I think it's about time we unpack a bit, shall we?"

The circle broke as the bunk scattered to unpack our respective bags. I breathed in relief; that wasn't as bad as I thought it would be. The first day was shaping up to be a good one, and it felt like it would hold for the rest of the session.

It could only get better from here.

Epilogue

I had one dollar left from the snack money Geshem had given us when we'd gone to see a baseball game earlier that summer. I held it close to me, anxious for a reason I couldn't place. I smoothed my dress and patted down my frizzy hair one last time before I stepped out of the bunk.

The sun was bright in the sky and it took me a minute to adjust my eyes. When I had, I looked around until I saw what I was looking for: a Chalutzimer, a member of the oldest age group at camp. He had a bouquet of carnations, like the one my dad had gotten for my mom almost thirty years earlier. I prepared my smile and walked up to the boy.

"Hi," I said, trying not to seem as uncomfortable as I was talking to an older camper I didn't know.

"Shabbat Shalom," he greeted.

"I'd like a carnation please," I said.

"Sure, which one?" He pushed the bouquet close enough to me that I could smell it. I hesitated, trying to remember which dress Talia had told me she would wear tonight. I wanted the flower to match.

"This one," I said, pulling out the fullest, deepest, reddest one in the bunch. I brought it to my nose to smell it, and I knew that I had made the right choice.

"That'll be $1.50."

I started sweating. "I thought it was only a dollar?" I asked nervously. It wouldn't be the end of the world if I couldn't give Talia the flower, but I wanted her to go home with something sweet to remember me by. I thought about my mom's prom corsage from my dad that she had pressed between the pages of a book.

"We didn't sell many last week," he said glumly. "We're trying to reach our tzedakah goal for the summer. It's going toward the rebuilding effort for that shul in Texas that was burned down."

I felt guilty; I hadn't known that it was for tzedakah. I thought about walking away but I didn't want him to think that I was greedy.

"I only have one dollar," I said sadly, handing the carnation back to him. "But you can have it." I handed him the dollar and began to walk away.

"Hey, wait!" he called to me after a few steps. I turned back to him.

"Take it," he insisted, reaching the flower out in my direction. I didn't move.

"You should have it. You're Reina, right?"

I instinctively took a step back. How did he know me? My heart was beating a little faster and the sun suddenly felt hotter.

"Yeah?" I half answered, half questioned.

"Then keep it," he said with a smile. "You're basically a legend in Chalutzim. Like ten kids came out after you got that rule changed."

I was flattered and embarrassed and guilty all at the same time. This kid didn't know me, but he knew that I was gay, which suddenly felt uncomfortably personal. But at the same time, he thought that I had changed the rule, which I hadn't, so I felt guilty. But in another way, I knew that I had helped in my way.

"I didn't do anything," I mumbled, taking back the flower and then looking down at my feet.

"Well, you were the first one who came out. They told us on like, the first day that someone in Chaverim had come out and that they changed the rule. Someone told me it was you. And then the next day, like ten kids came out as gay or bi or pan or whatever. One of my friends even said that he's nonbinary. I mean they," he corrected quickly. "We called it Yom Coming Out, like Yom Color War or Yom Camping."

"That's funny," I said, feeling calmer. "You know National Coming Out Day's a thing. It's like the non-Jewish version of Yom Coming Out."

"I know," he said with a goofy grin. "That's when I came out at school."

I grinned back. "I should get going," I said. "I'm meeting my girlfriend by the lake before Shabbos starts. I don't wanna be late!"

We waved at each other, and I started on my way, flower in hand, to go see Talia.

Acknowledgements and Thanks

Thank you to every queer camper and camper of color (and their parents) who told me their stories and encouraged me to write this book. Without your openness and willingness to share, this book wouldn't have been possible.

Thank you to my sensitivity readers who made sure this book is realistic and inoffensive; I hope you enjoyed the sneak peak!

Thank you to my amazing and supportive family, especially my parents, who have always supported me in my writing and in my life.

Thank you to my brother Avi who appointed himself my protector at camp in case anyone was homophobic toward me.

Finally, thank you to all of my counselors and the staff at Camp Ramah Palmer who worked to give me the best possible summers from Kochavim to Nivonim.

About the Author

Sarah L. Young is the author of *Nice Jewish Boys* (2017), *Plus One* (2018), and *Parsha Poetry* (2022). She began writing at 15 and hasn't stopped since. She earned her BA from Wellesley College in 2020 and her masters of fine arts in children's literature and writing for children from Simmons University in 2025. She currently resides in Boston.